FIREBASE

A NOVEL

of

WARTIME VIETNAM SUSPENSE
and ROMANCE

MARK ANTHONY SULLIVAN

Mark Anthony Sullivan
PO Box 386
Spring Lake, NJ 07762

This book is a work of fiction. Names, characters, places and incidents are products of the author's imagination or are used fictitiously, except for news reports of public figures and other actual media reports.

ISBN 978-0-9990507-0-5

Photo by manhhai.
https://www.flickr.com/photos/13476480@N07/30696966420

This book is dedicated to the men of Charlie Battery, 1st of the Fourteenth Artillery, Americal Division, in the words of our commander, Capt. Gary M. Biehl, "the finest artillery battery in Vietnam."

Chapter 1
HOME
SWEET FIREBASE

SP4 Michael Ward

Fire Support Base Las Vegas

Republic of Vietnam

May 17, 1970

Dear Sean,

The first thing they teach you in the army is how to make a bed—a lot of good that is doing me now. You can't make a bed if someone else is in it. There are ten men living in our bunker and just five folding canvas cots packed closely together. Only half the men can sleep at any one time. Not that that's a problem. At least five guys are always on duty in the fire direction center, which is in the same bunker. The FDC has to keep running twenty-four hours a day in case one of our infantry units gets attacked and needs supporting artillery fire. The gun crews have time to scramble while we're taking the radio call, but we have to start sticking pins in charts immediately in order to compute the firing data for the guns. Seconds can be crucial.

After landing in Vietnam almost two weeks ago, I was told I was assigned to the Twenty-Third Infantry Division out of Chu Lai. My first reaction was relief. Since I had never heard of the Twenty-Third Infantry Division, I figured it couldn't be doing anything too daring. Then I saw Chu Lai on the map and got a little worried. Everyone said the farther south you were, the safer you were. Chu Lai is pretty far north.

But the real surprise came on the plane from Long Binh. Most of the soldiers were wearing the well-known Southern Cross insignia of the Americal Division. I asked one of them why they were going to the headquarters of the Twenty-Third Infantry Division and was told that Twenty-Third Infantry Division is the Americal's numerical designation. The Americal Division! As much as I said I wanted to do my part, I'm not overjoyed at being assigned to the unit with the highest casualty rate in the war! At least I'm on a firebase and not in the field.

I arrived at the battery two days ago. We are located on Fire Support Base Las Vegas and are designated Charlie Battery, Second of the Ninety-Fifth Artillery. The base is located northwest of Chu Lai at the end of a long dirt road that is frequently mined by the Viet Cong. For that reason, the most important people come by helicopter. We came by truck.

I still feel like I'm just waking up from a dream. It's like when I went to sleep, I was a law student in New Jersey, and now I'm waking up as a soldier in Vietnam. I know what happened, but it all seems a blur. Up until two years ago, I just assumed I wouldn't have to worry about the draft until I graduated from law school. It was a shock when graduate school deferments got abolished. I had to enlist under a delayed program to avoid being pulled out of law school mid-semester, unless of course I accepted that Army Reserve appointment that the Wallaces lined up for me. Maybe I was stupid not to take it. Jane sure thought so, but with people our age without connections getting drafted, I just couldn't do that.

Even so, I didn't think I'd end up here. Most soldiers don't. The probability that I wouldn't have to leave the country kept Jane from exploding. She was even planning to move near whatever base I got assigned to. Once I got my orders for Vietnam, though, all bets were off.

I really didn't want to come here and didn't think I'd have to, but this is where I am now. I believe a lot of our fellow Americans are mistaken when they think we have nothing at stake. The communists took over Russia during World War I, not by popular vote but by military force. At the end of World War II, they took over Eastern Europe, not by popular vote but by military force. Eleven years ago they took over Cuba, not by popular vote but by military force. Now they are attempting to do the same thing in Vietnam by military force, without any election. I agree with the experts who say that the communist system is economically unsustainable, but by the time it collapses, it may have the whole world looking down the wrong end of a gun barrel. That is, unless we do something about it.

This is not the best time to be coming here. Our troop numbers have been dropping since early 1968, when they were at their peak. We have to be more cautious and alert than ever because our numbers keep getting smaller and smaller.

While we were in Chu Lai, we did our "in-country training" for a week. The most interesting part for me was the counter-sapper training, maybe because I knew I was going to a firebase. Sapper attacks are the classic form of assault on an artillery position that's surrounded by barbed wire. The demonstrations were done by actual captured North Vietnamese sappers. The wire used here is called concertina wire and comes in large coils about four feet in diameter. Two coils are stretched out like a spring and laid side by side. Then a third one is put on top to hold it up higher. The whole base is ringed in this way.

The North Vietnamese sapper prisoners showed us how they use their hands in the dark to feel around the coils for trip wires. Instead of cutting the barbed

wire, they press the coils apart and then tie them to
the outside coils to open a path. Their purpose is
to sneak in without alerting anyone. Once they are
inside, they work in teams of three. Two carry satchel
charges to throw into the bunkers, and one covers the
others with an AK-47 automatic rifle. The explosions
signal the other NVA outside the wire to commence
mortar fire, hoping to catch the defenders in the open
trying to respond to the blasts. More stressful but less
relevant for me was the tunnel training. For that we
had to crawl through dirt tunnels dug by hand by
other NVA prisoners.

The bunker we live and work in is half underground and made of a wood frame covered with sandbags. While they do provide protection from mortars,
the sandbags also absorb a lot of heat from the sun
during the day. At night, it's like sleeping and working
in an oven. You can't wear a shirt inside; it would soak
through with sweat in no time. The same is true with
socks. We all wear our boots over bare feet. Otherwise,
we'd get foot rot. Please excuse the smudges on the
paper. They're caused by the same thing. I remember reading in a magazine that journalists who work
in Vietnam teach themselves to piss just once a day
to avoid dehydration, but I don't think anyone here
could piss more than once a day no matter how hard
they tried. You just can't keep enough fluid in your
body for that.

I don't know that Mom and Dad would be

comfortable with everything here, so don't show them my letters. Just say it's brother stuff.

As ever,

Mike

SP4 Michael Ward

Fire Support Base Las Vegas

Republic of Vietnam

May 17, 1970

Dear Mom and Dad,

Well, I've arrived at my permanent station. The name of the post is Fire Support Base Las Vegas, but I can't seem to find either a roulette wheel or a floor show. Apart from that, the setup here is okay. We work in a deep bunker where we also have our sleeping quarters. In addition, there is a mess hall where we get three regular meals a day and they show movies at night. I used wooden ammunition boxes to make myself a locker and hung it on the wall in the sleeping part of the bunker. That's what everyone does here to store things. We have an electric generator to operate our radios and the FADAC (that's what we call the field artillery digital automatic computer). This also powers a small refrigerator in the hallway between the two rooms of the bunker.

The fire direction center where I work has two shifts, noon to midnight and midnight to noon. We have to be up and running to take radio calls at all times. I'm currently on midnight to noon, but that changes from time to time. My present job involves sticking pins in charts and taking measurements with an odd-looking device we call an RDP (which stands for range deflection protractor). Our fire direction officer, Lt. Barnes, says he's going to move me to the radio soon.

I had quite an odyssey getting here. After landing at Bien Hoa (pronounced Ben Wa) Airport, we were taken by bus convoy to Long Binh (Long Bin), where I was told I was going to Cu Chi (Coo Chee) and put on a plane. When I arrived at Cu Chi, they had no idea who I was. They checked and found out I was really supposed to go to Chu Lai (Chew Lie), head-quarters of the Twenty-Third Infantry Division. I had to ride back to Long Binh on a bus that had bars on the windows to protect against hand grenades. From there, I flew to Chu Lai. All of these big bases are well fortified and have facilities for beer, movies, and swimming. In Chu Lai we stayed in barracks on the beach looking out on the South China Sea. I pulled one night of guard duty there watching the water. No North Vietnamese ships got by me!

While in Chu Lai, I was processed through per-sonnel and told that I'm supposed to leave Vietnam on May 3, 1971. That's my DEROS date, which stands for date eligible for return from overseas. All of us, the new guys, were paid and awarded the Vietnam Service

Medal. The minute you step off the plane, you're entitled to that.

I was also told I'll be separated from the service immediately upon returning from Vietnam; I won't have to wait for my enlistment to run out. That's good. My last few days in the stateside army did not further endear them to me. After we reported to Oakland Army Base, we were issued our tropical gear. Our jungle fatigues are the usual olive drab color. Instead of shirts, though, we have what they call bush jackets, so called because they hang outside our pants. We were each issued two pairs of jungle boots. Only the toe and the heel are leather. The rest of the boot is green canvas, supposedly to allow in more air. There are flexible aluminum plates in the sole to protect against a type of booby trap called punji sticks. I had to wait until I got to battalion headquarters at LZ Bayonet to get my helmet, M-16 rifle, and flak jacket.

The last twenty-four hours before we left Oakland for Travis Air Force Base, we were locked down in a warehouse with bunk beds. I don't know why they thought all these soldiers who'd made it from all over the country to Oakland on their own were going to disappear between there and the airbase, but why does the army do anything? The warehouse was loaded with vending machines serviced by the rudest civilians I've ever seen. They were constantly telling the soldiers to get out of their way and insinuating that we were all too stupid to understand them. I wonder how they would have done at Holy Cross.

After all of that, the firebase almost seems like a home of sorts. The evenings feel cool outside after the sun goes down, and the officers and NCOs are friendly even with the enlisted men, a big change from the army in the States.

Love,

Mike

SP4 Michael Ward

Fire Support Base Las Vegas

Republic of Vietnam

May 20, 1970

Dear Mom & Dad,

I know you could not have gotten my letter yet with the address but I thought I'd keep you up to date on what's happening. May is a hot time of year here. We don't wear shirts inside our bunker since we're dripping with sweat. Fortunately, we can usually shower. Every few days they fly a water trailer out to us. It is positioned on a hill just above a small hut that has shower spigots. Presto, we have a shower room—sort of. Sometimes, like now, it doesn't work, so we have these portable showers. They're like five-gallon canvas buckets we hang on anything high enough. The bottom of the bucket has a shower head that twists on and off. You never know what the army has in its back pocket.

I was able to get a camera from the PX in Chu Lai. One of our cooks picked it up for me. They get in there more than we do. I took some pictures in FDC. Kodak Processing will send them home to you. The film here comes with envelopes to mail it to Kodak. Unfortunately, I'm not in the pictures. I took them. There's one of Edwin Smart, Doug Grayson, and Jim Kallin (left to right.)

I'm going to be ordering a component stereo system from PACEX over the course of this year. PACEX is the Pacific Exchange. Only service members in the Pacific theater are allowed to order from it. The prices are great. Everyone orders one piece at a time. I can get a turntable, a tape deck, a receiver, speakers, etc. I'm looking forward to having a great stereo system when I get home. Miss you.

Love,

Mike

Mrs. Patrick Ward

Jersey City, New Jersey

May 24, 1970

Michael dear,

I flew with you in spirit every mile of the way and trusted that you were in God's care and as comfortable as possible under the circumstances. This letter is being written so that I'll have one ready to mail as soon as I get your address. I have cleaned your room but have not tackled your mountain of records. That will have to wait until you return. I prayed for you at eight-thirty Mass this morning.

Joe and his fiancée, Cathy, had a party the other night, but Sean said it was no fun. Everyone felt your absence. Your Godmother Marjorie says she prays for you daily. She has had her own little altar set up on the dresser in her bedroom for some time. Now she is keeping a candle for you on it. (I hope it's not lit too often, considering her age and attention span.)

I saw Jane coming out of the drugstore on Monticello Avenue the day after you left. She was very pale and stuttered trying to say hello. She must have come down with something. I guess that's why she couldn't get to the airport when you left, but I didn't want to bother her with questions like that. She needs to spend a couple of days in bed and probably have some soup as well. Be sure to ask how she is.

The civilian clothes you sent back from San Francisco arrived yesterday. We did not expect them to be accompanied by an enormous stuffed puppy. Thank you. It has a prominent place in the den. At its size, it needs one.

We seem to be hearing from so many people who have children in Vietnam. Mrs. Fitzpatrick said that Charlie is there. Rick Zamia is there. Mrs. Allude, at the bank, said her son is there. Mrs. Hickey said her daughter Patricia is living in Saigon and working as a nurse. She gave me her address in case you got to Saigon, but I explained that you were in a more remote area. On the other hand, Dr. Smothers said his son Arnold would have nothing to do with the war. He acts as if he's the noble one. On a more positive note, nearly twenty-five hundred students at the University of Maine, including many war protesters, tried to donate blood to servicemen in Vietnam. There were so many they couldn't process all of them.

Lots of love,

Mom

Sean Ward

Jersey City, New Jersey

May 25, 1970

Hey Mike,

I thought I'd be starting my first letter to you with "How are things in Southeast Asia?" Don't worry, I'll get to that, but it's been a very strange month. How will historians explain it? First, the president sends troops into Cambodia, and then the Ohio National Guard kills four students at Kent State University. Then we have construction workers beating up protesters in Manhattan. I don't even know what my own thoughts are yet. While I think the Cambodia thing was a mistake, I'm not sure. Could it shorten the war? Maybe, but whatever position people take, I wish they would think about it before they open their mouths. The silent majority doesn't analyze; it just supports whatever the president does. The opponents aren't much different. To them, whatever Nixon does is always wrong. Strangely, the students killed did not appear to come from this radical group. One girl was just on her way to class.

I went to a dinner party at Jack and Vivian's house last week. Some of the guests were so adamant that the demonstrators got what they deserved from the construction workers that it made no sense to even try to discuss the issue with them. I just kept my mouth closed for the rest of the meal.

All of that aside, how *are* things in Southeast Asia? I saw your letter to Mom and Dad, but it sounded a little sterile. I'll wait to see when I get one, which I imagine you've already sent. I can well imagine that what's happening here now may seem far removed to you, but let's get something straight. You have just one important thing to do now, and that is to make sure you get home alive and well. Nothing else matters. You're not there to prove anything, let alone to win the war by yourself.

Do you mind telling me what's going on with Jane? Obviously everyone noticed that she didn't join us at Newark Airport to see you off to Oakland. We just didn't want to say anything at that point. It was stressful enough as it was. I know you had dinner with her the night before. Now Donna at Luigi's is telling us Jane stormed out of the restaurant, knocking over a bottle of wine. She didn't even stop to apologize. If it's none of my business, just say so.

Take care of yourself,

Sean

SP4 Michael Ward

Fire Support Base Las Vegas

Republic of Vietnam

May 28, 1970

Dear Mom & Dad,

They do have movies here at Firebase Las Vegas. Last night it was *How to Commit Marriage* with Bob Hope and Jackie Gleason. Most of the soldiers watch the movie in the mess hall after dinner once it's dark enough. We can't show movies outside here like they do on the big bases. It would be too easy for the enemy to see us. As it is, we have to keep the windows blacked out. Those of us on the FDC noon-to-midnight shift can't go to that showing, so we run it again afterwards. Other guys come to that showing as well, including those who had been on guard duty and gun crews who were shooting H&Is during the earlier showing.

H&I stands for harassment and interdiction. Several times a night, we fire one gun at a location from which the VC are likely to launch rockets at Chu Lai.

We don't select the location; battalion does. I have no idea whether it's effective or not, but it does use up a lot of ammunition. We put out a little over three hundred rounds a day, and most of them are H&Is.

It takes a while to learn to sleep here. It's not just the heat; mostly it's the noise. Our 105mm howitzers are about fifty meters from our bunker, and the 155mm howitzers of the other battery are two hundred meters away but are much louder. Most of the shooting is done at night. The longer you are here, though, the less you notice it.

Why is a group in New York called Artists on Strike proposing a citywide shutdown of galleries and museums to protest "war, racism, and political repression"? Do they think that having been deprived of fine art, racists will suddenly see the light and begin to treat all people fairly, that political tyrants will just wither away without art to nourish them, or that locking the museum door will force warring parties to the peace table? It's gotten to the point where the urge to protest seems to outweigh common sense. At least the Metropolitan Museum of Art and the Museum of Modern Art have refused to participate.

Love,

Mike

Mrs. Patrick Ward

Sea Girt, New Jersey

May 30, 1970

Michael dear,

It is a lovely, lazy afternoon with a soft breeze blowing through the trees. Tuesday was not a nice day, but the arrival of your letter changed all that. More importantly, in two more days I can cross May off the calendar and move onto June, one month closer to your coming home.

I recently read that the board of education in Las Vegas is opening a new school where classes will begin at 5:00 p.m. This is to accommodate the large number of parents there who work nights. I don't think I'd want to be a teacher there—although with scheduling like that, it appears that your firebase has more in common with Las Vegas than just its name.

We are staying at the shore just for the weekend now but will be here more often once the summer really begins. School will end in about two more weeks. I'm staying busy moving the lawn sprinkler around. The lilacs are beautiful, and Dad has put in the tomato plants. They seem to be thriving. There was a cookout at the Spring Lake Golf Club last night with steaks and lobster outside and a buffet table inside. It was wonderful. Next year, you'll be there, too. While we were standing at the grill on the patio waiting for our meat to cook, we were talking to the Boyds, who were anxious to hear all about you and your present setup. Your father is back at the club now playing golf.

Lots of love,

Mom

Patrick Ward

Jersey City, New Jersey

June 3, 1970

Dear Mike,

We were happy to get your address so we could start writing. That was quite a time you had getting to your duty station. Once you get settled there, we would like to get all the details. From what you say so far, your setup does not seem that bad. Be careful though. I remember reading a few months back that a large Viet Cong hospital had been found just fifteen miles west of Chu Lai, so the area is not safe.

The New Jersey Supreme Court came down with an important ruling Monday reversing a superior court decision in Hudson County. The lower court had ordered the police to destroy all intelligence files on civil rights activists and other protesters. That order was overruled in a unanimous decision written by Chief Justice Weintraub. The ACLU is all up in arms, saying it will appeal to the United States Supreme Court, because the court "did not understand the scope or depth of the issue involved."

Your mother and I were happy to learn you'll be getting out of the army as soon as you come home. We hope you will go back to law school then. Your work reminds me of what we did in the navy. We took a lot of measurements on charts too, only we were looking for U-boats. Don't worry about the clowns with the vending machines. They'll still be there when you're admitted to the bar.

Affectionately,

Dad

Mrs. Patrick Ward

Sea Girt, New Jersey

June 5, 1970

Michael dear,

I was walking home from school when Henry the mailman told me there was a letter waiting at the house from you. That certainly speeded up my pace. Dad and I were packing up to come down here, but we made sure to devour your missive first.

Althea Foxx stopped in to see us yesterday. She was up for the Junior League luncheon. She looks so marvelous it's hard to believe how old she is. Of all things, she was complaining about how dull it is in Washington now, that the social life there has just collapsed. Maybe it's just as well that the government has its mind on things other than parties.

We just arrived here, having stopped at several garden centers on the way. We bought little bushes and beautiful hanging plants for the porch. There is no time to fix dinner, so we are going over to the golf club. (A much better idea anyway!)

Joan O'Mara's fiancé, Robert, stopped by the other day. As you know, he was in the artillery in Vietnam. He assured me that you're much safer on a firebase than you would be as a forward observer. I said you'd be safer still back in law school.

We're past our normal dinnertime, so I should get going.

Love,

Mom

Mrs. Patrick Ward

Jersey City, New Jersey

June 11, 1970

Michael dear,

It's 10:20 a.m. and my students are working on a long test, which means they're quiet and I have time to write. Last night we went to Greenbrook Country Club for a dinner party the Wallaces gave for the Boyds. It was a lovely affair. Everything was superbly done. There was a marvelously talented guitar player. He sang in four languages. I can't tell you, though, how many people were shocked to learn that you were in Vietnam.

I just got home from school a little while ago and have taken this letter out again to finish. It's very hot, so I took some iced tea out to the men working on the telephone pole in the back. In two weeks, we have to go up to your cousin Theresa's wedding in Maine.

As the school year winds down, I am starting to get presents from some of the students. In the past, the gifts have usually been things for me to use, like soap or gloves. This year, most of the students (their parents, really) are enrolling you in prayer societies instead. People of every race, color, and creed will be praying for you. Keep up your spirits, dear. We are all praying for you too.

Lots of love,

Mom

SP4 Michael Ward

Fire Support Base Las Vegas

Republic of Vietnam

June 11, 1970

Dear Sean,

A truck got blown up by a land mine on our dirt road early this morning. It was the front right tire that set the device off, so the guy in the passenger seat was badly hurt but not killed. We could hear the explosion here, so two of our jeeps raced out loaded with guys with M-16s, but nothing more happened. I called for a medevac helicopter.

Now that the US is withdrawing its troops, a lot of guys here think the NVA and Viet Cong are going to sit back and wait until we're completely gone before launching any major offensives. I hope they're right, but I really don't believe they are—especially when stuff keeps happening, stuff like this morning. As our troop strength gets weaker and weaker, we should be getting more and more careful, not the opposite.

The real question in my mind, though, is who is doing this. We're not in the jungle. We're two miles from Route 1. All the villages here are located along it, with rice paddies extending west around our base. US Army vehicles are driving up and down Route 1 all the time, right through the villages. The VC and NVA are certainly not going to send troops humping long distances through the mush of the rice paddies and the brush along the roadway just to plant mines. Someone around here has to be doing it, and I think I know how to find out who.

You asked about Jane. Yeah, what Donna said was true. I haven't heard anything since. I just don't know.

Take care,

Mike

Chapter 2
HELLO AGAIN

Patrick Ward

Jersey City, New Jersey

June 12, 1970

Dear Mike,

I'm trying to clean up that balance scale we found to put on the desk in my office. It looks enough like the scales of justice to be appropriate at a law school. By the way, I've been asked to prepare and teach a continuing legal education course to judges and practicing attorneys on dealing with the deliberate disruption of court proceeding by parties or their lawyers. As you probably notice from reading the news, this is becoming a favorite tactic of some of the radical left wing groups. Instead of trying to win a case, they misbehave and disrupt the courtroom proceedings to the point that it prejudices the outcome and leads to reversal on appeal. Trial judges need to walk a very fine line between getting their backs up and overreacting on one hand and catering too much to the miscreants on the other. Some don't seem to be very good at it. Just holding someone in contempt of court doesn't help much.

The camera was a good idea. It's easier to get a Japanese one where you are than it is here. Also, sending the pictures home is smarter than trying to keep them there in the heat.

I'm still having trouble figuring out exactly where you are. Is it near Danang? Aunt Anne is not doing well. Her cancer has progressed to the point where she can't get out at all. It's only a matter of time.

Affectionately,

Dad

Jane O'Brien

Jersey City, New Jersey

June 13, 1970

Dear Michael,

Why did I have to find out your address from your mother? I know, I know! We didn't part on the best of terms, but couldn't you have written me anyway? I'm still your girlfriend, okay? I may hate that you are where you are. I may hate that you joined the regular army when you were offered a spot in the reserves, and I certainly hate being alone, but it's only because I love you too much to just sit back and accept it.

What made it even worse, though, was having to admit I hadn't even heard from you. Your mother sounded a little dumbfounded on the phone that I had to call her for your address, and she assured me that keeping in contact with me was something you'd never overlook. She went on to explain that the mail service from Vietnam is anything but regular and that letters don't necessarily arrive in the order they are sent. You and I both know that wasn't the problem.

Where are you, anyway? These army APO addresses don't tell very much. Your mom says it's a firebase. What's that? Is it big, little? Are you in the jungle? What are they giving you to eat? Please tell me what's happening.

In the meantime, I can tell you a few things. It seems I have full-time job. One of the older teachers at Clarence Elementary became ill. The details are not clear, but I've picked up her class for the remainder of this school year and will continue in September. It's third grade. So far everyone is nice. I think I'll be happy there. I love kids, as you well know! And the timing couldn't have been better. I was still free so we could spend your whole thirty-day leave together and even get away to South Carolina. It's remembering that trip keeps me from going crazy. Michael, that was just eight weeks ago. How did we end up like this?

At least you got over there too late to have to go into Cambodia. I hope Tricky Dick doesn't have any more of these stunts up his sleeve. Right now there seems to be more chaos here than where you are. There have been strikes at universities all over the country. Final exams have been canceled almost everywhere, and Kent State was unbelievable, American soldiers shooting American students. You don't have to go to Vietnam to be in a wringer, but anyway, keep your head down and don't do anything brave or stupid.

Please write to me. I'm not looking forward to this summer at all. Most of all, just stay safe.

Love (really),

Jane

SP4 Michael Ward

Fire Support Base Las Vegas

Republic of Vietnam

June 14, 1970

Dear Mom & Dad,

So far today I've been working on our meteorological data. It is different for us than it was in earlier wars. In a conventional war, artillery was fired in one direction only, toward the enemy. If the target was somewhere other than straight ahead, they had to use wind cards to adjust for the change of direction. The distance the projectile travels is affected not just by wind but also by the rotation of the earth. A shot fired west will go farther than one fired east, just like the sun appears to move from east to west. In both cases though, it's really the movement of the earth that factors in.

In a guerilla war like this, however, we have to be prepared to shoot in any direction. So we have what's called an eight-directional met message, which we receive four times a day. It's really a fancy name for a weather report, but every time we receive it, we have to calculate what effect it will have on every one of eight directions in a full circle. Whenever we receive the grid coordinates of a new target, we have to look and see which one of the eight directions it is closest to, determine the proper adjustment, and draw a thin pencil line on our slide rule to allow for it. It's usually very small, but when you're shooting close to your own troops, small adjustments can be critical.

Fortunately, we don't have to worry about everyday paraphernalia here such as toothpaste or shaving cream. We get SP packs regularly. SP stand for sundries pack. In addition to tooth brushing and shaving stuff, it includes candy, cigarettes, even chewing tobacco, although we seem to accumulate a lot of that, as no one uses it. The chocolate bars are called tropical chocolate because they don't melt. It also makes them hard to eat. The soldiers refer to them as "John Wayne bars." They don't issue SP packs in rear areas, as the guys there have access to a PX.

It's hard to keep track of all the strife back home like Muhammad Ali's appeal of his conviction for draft evasion and the attempt to impeach Justice Douglas.

The one big change that seems to have caused no controversy here is the appointment of the army's first two women generals. Gen. Westmoreland presided over the ceremony, which was attended by Mamie Eisenhower. One of the new generals had taken care of President Eisenhower at Walter Reed Army Hospital.

Love,

Mike

SP4 Michael Ward

Fire Support Base Las Vegas

Republic of Vietnam

June 20, 1970

Dear Jane,

I'm sorry I didn't write sooner, but I didn't think you wanted me to. Actually I did write you a letter, but I tore it up instead of mailing it. After what happened at Luigi's, I didn't know what to think. The last I saw of you was your back running out the door, leaving a smashed bottle of wine on the floor behind. After you didn't show up at Newark Airport, the last thing I thought you would want was a letter from me. Your not being there was at least as rough for me as my not writing was for you.

I can't go back in time. Even if I could, something would still bother me about accepting a reserve appointment when guys my age who don't have "ins" are getting drafted. Make no mistake, the only thing I look forward to is getting back to you. Sometimes it's all I can think about. But after what happened, I wasn't sure where you stood. No one I've met wants to be here, but our country did take on this commitment, and it's not fair to cast off its burden only onto people with poor connections. Anyway, what can I do now?

This is a small firebase. That means we have guns here, howitzers, which are a type of cannon. We're not in the jungle. We're surrounded by rice paddies. I live in a bunker covered with sandbags. I'm okay. I'm glad about your job.

I do feel terrible about the students who were killed at Kent State. While their antics may have gotten out of hand, soldiers should never shoot into a crowd like that. There are so many other effective riot control techniques and formations that National Guardsmen can use, and they should be familiar with them. In a riot situation, gunfire should be used only on specifically identified and dangerous targets such as snipers or fire bombers.

Completely leaving aside the question of whether the US should stay in Vietnam, it seems to me as long as we do stay here, we can't allow the North Vietnamese to have sacrosanct supply lines running through "neutral" countries. That is why I have trouble understanding the outcry in the Senate about expanding the war. I could understand wanting to bring us home, but I cannot understand their telling us we have to stay here but at the same time saying we can't protect ourselves by interrupting the shipment of the enemy's war materials, weapons, and ammunition. We're not trying to conquer Cambodia, go to war with it, or fight it in any way. We're simply trying to stop the North Vietnamese from using the Ho Chi Minh Trail as their own little private highway that no one else is allowed to interfere with. We didn't expand the war to Cambodia; we're trying to keep it out of Cambodia.

Spending my thirty-day leave together with you was nice, no matter how it ended. We're lucky to live in New Jersey with so many romantic Italian restaurants. You look beautiful in candlelight, especially when the candle is stuck in a wine bottle. I so miss seeing it. Please keep writing!

Love,

Mike

SP4 Michael Ward

Fire Support Base Las Vegas

Republic of Vietnam

June 20, 1970

Dear Sean,

I must have lost my mind. Jim Kallin, one of my buddies here in FDC, certainly thought I had, but here's what happened. Yesterday after dinner, I asked Jim to follow me down the dirt road. It stays light later this time of year, so the firebase entrance and perimeter were not secured yet. The road is lined by heavy brush on both sides, higher than a man's head. About a mile down the roadway, a path leads into it.

I followed the path but asked Jim to stay about twenty feet behind me. We were both armed with M-16s. It seemed unlikely to me that anyone we found would be that well armed. They may have had a mine to plant, but I did not think the VC would let local villagers in this area keep AK-47s. They would be too likely to be discovered. What would they use them for, anyway? They didn't expect to fight anyone, only to plant explosives.

What we came across were a half dozen what I will call junior-high-school-aged boys all around fourteen years old. They were surprised to see us, but they immediately took out some pornographic black-and-white pictures from their pockets and tried to sell them to us, as if this would explain what they were doing hiding in the brush just before dark right next to a roadway that frequently got mined. We didn't see any weapons or mines, but I suspect something was there. Even if they were not the mine planters, which is unlikely, they had to be brushing shoulders with them. They couldn't speak English, and we can't speak Vietnamese. As a practical matter, there was nothing we could do except leave.

I guess all that we did was to enlighten ourselves about what's really happening here. These kids were obviously local. The people here must know who they are and what they're doing. That can only mean a large portion of the people we think we're defending are in fact either against us or are at least playing both sides of the street. Jim was adamant that we not tell any of the officers or NCOs what we found. They wouldn't have been able to do anything, either, except come down hard on us. FDC personnel are not supposed to go looking for VC in the bush. I even wonder how good our own infantry would be at this. Wouldn't the South Vietnamese Army be a lot more effective in dealing with problems like this? Not only do they speak the language, but a lot of them come from villages just like this and understand them a lot better than we ever could.

As ever,

Mike

Jane O'Brien

Spring Lake, New Jersey

June 22, 1970

Dear Michael,

Have I been leading you into a life of crime? Did you know that New Jersey has a 179-year-old law prohibiting "sexual intercourse with an unmarried woman"? Really, they convicted someone of it recently, the first time in the history of the law! Is this supposed to be progress?

Leaving our conspiracy aside, I'm taking the summer off, going to the beach and reading. New Jersey is good for that. Some of my new friends from work tried to get me to go in on a group rental in Belmar with them, but I had no desire to get beer poured over me in the middle of the night, so I'm staying at my parents' summer place. The rent is just perfect, and I sometimes get meals too. Of course, you have all the free rent and free meals you can handle right now, but I don't think it's the same.

I've been enjoying the movies too. *Butch Cassidy and the Sundance Kid* was good, and Walter Matthau was so funny in *Cactus Flower.* So far I've only been out one night to a bar, Jimmy Byrne's. It was okay. I enjoy talking to my friends but do get annoyed by some of the overconfident would-be Romeos. Don't worry, I know how to get rid of them. Since you went away, I've learned how to act like a real bitch. Now, if you were here, I wouldn't have to do that, would I?

Love,

Jane

Patrick Ward

Sea Girt, New Jersey

June 23, 1970

Dear Mike,

The Yankees–Red Sox game Sunday at Fenway Park turned into a real thriller, twenty-four runs and thirty-eight hits. The game went eleven innings and lasted four hours. In that last inning, however, the Yankees scored six runs, and it was over. There were 31,073 people at the stadium.

Exactly how big is this facility where you're located? Are there many people there? Are they all artillery, or are there other branches as well? I imagine you would have to have some infantry there for security, as the men in your unit can't both man the big, long-distance guns and defend your own base at the same time.

The big legal news around here is the Black Panthers trial at the Hudson County Court House. It involves a machine-gun attack on a police station. In a recent turn of events, the defendants have subpoenaed two *New York Times* reporters, Walter Waggoner and Francis Clines, to testify at the trial. It's hard to tell what they want from them, but I can foresee this raising all kinds of constitutional issues.

Your mother is finished for the school year, and I am not teaching any classes this summer, so we'll be staying down here most of the time. They still haven't gotten rid of that ship that sailed onto the beach last year. If it stays any longer, they'll have to declare it a historic site and put a sign on it.

Affectionately,

Dad

Mrs. Patrick Ward

Sea Girt, New Jersey

June 23, 1970

Michael dear,

Today is a lovely June day, temperature in the seventies. It may not be suitable for the beach, but it's perfect for the garden. I went to Guinco's today and bought lamb chops for tonight. Your father is going to cook them on the charcoal grill in the backyard. I am going to do the baked potatoes in the oven. We have a nice bottle of red wine to go with them. Don't worry, next summer, you'll be here sharing with us.

According to an article I read in the *Times,* for fifteen years now, no state has lowered its voting age. Proposals to do so have consistently been rejected by the voters. The article goes on to say that the reason for this is that those voters, who are over twenty-one, are distressed by recent campus unrest. Over twenty-one! More like over fifty-one!

Fine, I have my own proposal. There should be a new law that only people eligible to vote are allowed to serve in the armed forces. Then all these older people who believe that eighteen-year-olds are not responsible enough to cast a ballot but are responsible enough to have to walk around rice paddies with a rifle can take their places in the front lines.

Lots of love,

Mom

SP4 Michael Ward

Fire Support Base Las Vegas

Republic of Vietnam

June 24, 1970

Dear Sean,

I have a story to tell you. It's been blistering hot all week, and we've had a lot of work to do outside in the sun when we're not on duty in FDC. Capt. Berlen, our new battery commander, felt that the cover of sandbags on the FDC bunker wasn't thick enough and ordered us to add two more layers.

During one of our late-night shifts several weeks ago, Jim Kallin and I got to talking about martinis. It had been a long time since either of us had had one, so we agreed that whichever of us next went into Chu Lai would bring back a bottle of gin and one of dry vermouth, and we would split the cost. It's not much at the PX. As it turns out, Jim went earlier this week and brought back the stuff. We poured a little of the vermouth into his canteen, filled it halfway with gin, shook it up, and poured in the rest of the gin. Since we have an electric generator to run the radio and the lights, we also have a small refrigerator. We put the canteen in there, with Jim's name grease-penciled on it.

It was over a hundred degrees as we worked outside putting the sandbags on the roof. Damon Williams, a strict Southern Baptist who had never had a drink in his life, was feeling parched and his canteen was empty, so he decided to drink from Jim's. He took a big, long gulp and then let out the worst yell I've ever heard. He went down on one knee and looked as if he were going to collapse. Even I have trouble imagining what it would feel like to swallow that much martini in one slug, and I'm used to drinking martinis. Jim didn't see it happen. He was over at the latrine, so I told Damon what it was. I hope we didn't start him on the path to ruin, but at least we cured him from drinking from someone else's canteen without asking.

The more I read the news, the more I feel that this may really be a good time to be away from the United States. Some reports say that America is facing its worst domestic crisis since the Civil War: race riots, students being shot by troops on campus, colleges and universities canceling final exams. What's happening? Some reports even say that American universities will cease to exist. Lucky me to be in Vietnam!

As ever,

Mike

SP4 Michael Ward

Fire Support Base Las Vegas

Republic of Vietnam

June 26, 1970

Dear Sean,

I never did much thinking about the American flag much before coming here. Of course I've done the stuff we all did: recited the Pledge of Allegiance, sang the national anthem. As soldiers in training, we stood at attention and presented arms when the bugle played "To the Colors" and the flag was lowered. It's totally different now, though. All we have here is a barren dirt hilltop covered with sandbags. There is nothing but rice paddies all around us day in and day out. It would be the dreariest place on earth with no color at all but for that red, white, and blue banner. It stands out on the flagpole for me like it never did before. We may have passed identical flags without experiencing any emotion thousands of time in parks, in front of schools, in ball fields, and in stadiums. Here, however, it's the one thing that says who we are and why we came, the one thing that makes us something other than smelly men in dirty, sweat-soaked clothes. We can look up at it and say we really mean something and we were sent here on a mission on behalf of our homeland on the other side of the globe. I hope I'm not sounding too sanctimonious, but it's not something very many people understand.

As ever,

Mike

Jane O'Brien

Jersey City, New Jersey

June 27, 1970

Dear Michael,

You know what, let's just say we never fought at Luigi's. I don't want that place to have bad memories. We have too many good ones there. Remember when I spilled all that tomato sauce? Oh my God! Donna had to lend me a blouse to wear home. Maybe that's not the best incident to cite as a good memory, or maybe it is. I'd rather relive that day than this one. Tomato sauce is one thing you don't have to worry about where you are now.

Which reminds me, your letter was not a bundle of information about what's really happening. I learned more from talking to Sean than I did from reading your letter. Is everything okay? I'm not going to believe you if you say you have a comfortable bed, air conditioning, and a martini every night. Tell me the truth. Just because I wanted to whack you over the head for going there in the first place doesn't mean I don't worry about you every minute of every day. You brought part of me with you, even if it went kicking and screaming.

My job really is good. I so much like working with the kids. I'm making good friends, too. More of the new teachers are men than in the past. Some people say it's because teaching is draft-deferrable. I don't know. All of them are nice, though. There's Jim and Jeremy and Carol and Ann—or should I say Mr. Hughes, Mr. Hinkle, Miss Connell, and Miss Rica. You know how proper teachers are supposed to be. I don't have any real social life, and I'm certainly not dating anyone else, no matter what you think. I'll just read more. I need to do that anyway.

Did you see that the girl whose picture appeared in so many papers kneeling by one of the bodies at Kent State was a fourteen-year-old runaway? Her parents recognized her and notified the local police. Now she wants to go home to her family. It's no wonder. She had met the dead student only twenty-five minutes before he was shot. He was twenty. Oh, as far as the Ho Chi Minh Trail is concerned, the North Vietnamese can turn it into a paved highway with toll booths for all I care, as long as we get you and your friends home safely.

I'm enclosing a Miraculous Medal. Please keep it on you at all times. My father did in World War II, and he came back healthy. Pin it onto your underwear if you're not allowed to wear it anywhere else. Right now, it's the only way I have left to protect you.

Love,

Jane

Mrs. Patrick Ward

Jersey City, New Jersey

June 28, 1970

Michael dear,

This is one of those weekends that remind me that the Irish should never complain about cold, damp weather. That's what we came from. Still, a lot of people who are here for the weekend are not getting to enjoy the beach.

For more cheerful news, Dad loves the Vietnamese smoking jacket you sent him. He looks so elegant in it. We've had a number of invitations to go on trips recently, but we just don't feel up to it. Maybe once you come home. Can you get allergy shots where you are now? You know how much they were helping you.

I'm now off to Mass to pray for a certain GI.

Lots of love,

Mom

Jane O'Brien

Spring Lake, New Jersey

June 28, 1970

Dear Michael,

It's been a miserable weekend weather-wise, rain

yesterday, fog today. I did get to Mass this morning and prayed and prayed and prayed, and you know what for! Then I came home and tried to read but couldn't focus on anything because my thoughts were so wrapped up in you and me. I just started thinking about the summer two years ago. It was a normal summer. We had both graduated. I had that job at the hotel. You worked on the highway. We had plenty of time to spend together. How did a war get in the way? This wasn't supposed to happen to our generation.

For years I thought it was so romantic to see Humphrey Bogart and Ingrid Bergman dancing in Paris, reminiscing in Casablanca, and always running from the Nazis. I now know what Ilsa meant when she said she hated that war. I wonder what it was really like for the people in France during the occupation. They had a lot of internal division too. They had collaborators. They had resistance fighters. They were more violent than what we have, but Kent State was still scary! I know that you're far away from Saigon, but I still wonder what the intrigue must be like there.

I think I finally have some perception of what our parents lived through in World War II. While a lot of things are different, some never change. There's this feeling that your life plan has been distorted. You've lost control, and every day you wake up wondering if you'll get bad news. I've watched *Casablanca* four times and I'm sure I'll watch again, but the next time I know it's going to feel different.

Love,

Jane

Mrs. Patrick Ward

Jersey City, New Jersey

June 29, 1970

Michael dear,

We drove back here from Maine yesterday and are heading for the shore today. It was easier to break up the trip, plus there were things we could do in Jersey City. We did have dinner at The Alps last night, but it was quiet with so many people away. Theresa's wedding went very well. Lots of your Ward relatives were there. Of course, with Anne's condition being what it is, the Clarkes could not make it.

Everyone, and I mean everyone, wanted to hear about you. We were asked so many questions that we never got to talk about anything else. The weather was cool, in the fifties, but clear. The reception was at an old historic inn with cocktails outside. I was glad I brought a sweater.

Fifty-six percent of the population now feels that it was a mistake for the US to send troops into Vietnam. This is a big change from 1965, when only twenty-four percent felt it was a mistake. Does anyone really understand that we love and support our troops and at the same time wish they were not there?

Early on, people with college backgrounds were the most likely to support the war. Now, they are the most likely to oppose it.

Lots of love,

Mom

Jane O'Brien

Jersey City, New Jersey

June 30, 1970

Dear Michael,

I bought a new car. It's a Firebird, used, but only three years old and not much mileage. I needed something to get to work. Then yesterday, I couldn't get the key out of the ignition. Since I couldn't just leave it on the street that way, I drove right to the dealer, but the mechanic there was no help at all when I told him what it was. He said, "Can't you just get your boyfriend to fix it?" When I said that was impossible because you were in Vietnam, his whole attitude changed and he couldn't have been more helpful. (I didn't bother to tell him you probably couldn't have done much anyway.) But see, you did help with a mechanical problem even without being here! As a matter of fact, that might be the only benefit I'm likely to get from your being where you are.

I understand you're going to be working with a radio. As long as you're just talking, you should be fine. You could be a radio announcer or even a TV anchorman. I would love to watch you. As good as you might be at the speaking part, however, if the radio breaks, I hope they have someone else to repair it.

I ran into one of your old school friends the other day, Ed Sinnott. He had just had his draft board physical, which he failed for psychiatric reasons! Well, I always did think he seemed a little crazy, but maybe he's just clever and not as picky as you. Anyway, he was as happy as a clam at high tide.

Love,

Jane

SP4 Michael Ward

Fire Support Base Las Vegas

Republic of Vietnam

June 30, 1970

Dear Mom & Dad,

I was reading in *Stars and Stripes* the other day about a study done by the Rand Corporation that estimated a Viet Cong takeover of South Vietnam would result in reprisal killings of at least 100,000 people. The study is titled "Viet Cong Repression and Its Implications" and was released by the Pentagon on June 15. While I'm not overly inclined to believe every press release that comes out of the Defense Department, this one does ring true. As much as some of the war protesters like to portray the Viet Cong (who they always refer to as the National Liberation Front) as a bunch of Santa's elves in conical hats, we have only to look at what the North Vietnamese did in Hue in 1968 to realize how they would treat the South Vietnamese who had opposed them.

Love,

Mike

SP4 Michael Ward

Fire Support Base Las Vegas

Republic of Vietnam

June 30, 1970

Dear Jane,

I don't remember any argument at Luigi's, at least not anymore. All I remember is your face in the candlelight. I go to sleep thinking of it every night. When I get home, the first thing I want to do is to go back to Luigi's. Next time, we'll do it right.

I will carry the medal you sent, but I can't very well pin it to my underwear since we don't wear any. It is so hot inside the bunker that we can't. Any extra layers would be sweat-soaked in no time. We're listening to the radio right now—the one that plays music, not the other, although that's on too, as always. Edison Lighthouse is singing "Love Grows Where My Rosemary Goes." To date, life on this base hasn't been very scary, but it is monotonous. It's like we wear the same clothes every day, eat the same food every day, see the same few people every day. Sometimes it seems more like a prison than an armed camp.

Anyway, according to the army, we can now wear our hair longer. The way styles are going at home, it will still probably be easy to tell right away who's in the military and who's not just by the haircut. When I went to the barbershop before leaving home for Oakland, the man in the next chair, an older man, asked me if I was in the army and said he had been too. Then he said, "Like you, I was in the peacetime army." I'm not often rendered speechless.

My last stop before I came to this firebase was LZ Bayonet, where our battalion headquarters are located. It's a small base close to Chu Lai. I only got to spend one night there, but there was a club that served alcohol. It's the only liquor-serving facility I've ever been in that won't admit anyone unarmed. I hadn't been issued my M-16 yet, so I had to borrow an M-79 grenade launcher from one of the guys in the headquarters crew to get in for a drink. Vietnam sure is a different kind of place!

Love,

Mike

SP4 Michael Ward

Fire Support Base Las Vegas

Republic of Vietnam

June 30, 1970

Dear Sean,

Yesterday we did a time on target, a technique for clearing a landing zone of enemy troops to permit our helicopters to land. The idea is to have several batteries from different bases firing at the same target in such a way that the first rounds from each of the batteries all hit the ground simultaneously, creating one massive explosion. It's easier than it sounds. Our slide rules, which are called GFTs (graphic firing tables), do show the time of flight from the gun to the target. Battalion gives us the time on target, the time when all the first rounds are supposed to impact, after which we subtract the time of flight. I had to coordinate all the batteries by telling each one when to fire (time on target minus their particular time of flight) and counting backward over the radio up to time on target, so that we're all working from the same watch. Once we finish, helicopter gunships give the zone another going-over with rockets. Then the slicks land with the troops. This is supposed to keep them from landing into an ambush. It seems to work.

Living conditions here are still not the greatest. Our toilets consist of fifty-gallon drums cut in half. Periodically, they are filled with gasoline and set on fire to sanitize them. It's just one more example of the army's way of doing things! Another problem is that all our bunkers are infested with rats. Our FDC bunker has canvas cots that keep us off the floor, so it's a little better for us. The gun crews' bunkers have bunk beds built into the walls. They're just wooden shelves with air mattresses, which permit the rats to run across them at night. We do have a lot of rat traps set, baited with licorice candy from the SP packs. We catch a lot of rats. The other day, we had a rat so big the trap didn't kill him, and he got out of it. He was over a foot long, and the base of his tail was almost an inch in diameter. We didn't want to shoot at him in the bunker, so we bayoneted him. I didn't even know they made bayonets for M-16s, but we had one. The ring on the bayonet was so large that the whole thing looked awkward, but it had to be to get around the flash suppressor on an M-16.

We deal a lot with our battalion FDC. All our fire missions are worked up twice, once by us and once by the battalion FDC crew. We won't shoot unless the figures agree. In effect, the firing data gets worked up four times, because both FDCs do it on the FADAC computer as well as on the slide rules. The computer is somewhat slow, so we can always do the data faster on the slide rules. I suspect that will change as the technology progresses. Battalion FDC is run by the S3, which is what they call the operations officer. At division level, the operations officer is called the G3, since that's general staff.

With all the concern here about security against sapper attacks, it occurred to me that it might be helpful to have a few dogs on the base. If nothing else, they might bark if they sensed sappers in or inside our wire. I suggested that to Lt. Barnes. His response was, "Do you know what an army dog costs? Ten thousand dollars!" I pointed out that we didn't need a ten-thousand-dollar trained army dog, just a mutt from the village we could probably buy for five bucks. He would have none of it. One of the guys from the other shift was walking through and chimed in, "There's no need for that shit anymore. We haven't had a single guy in this battery killed so far this year. Last year we had eight. The gooks know we're leaving anyway and don't want to bother with us." He's been here nine months, but I don't think I'd want him covering my back.

I'm not sure what is going on with the Gulf of Tonkin Resolution. Why is Congress voting to repeal it? Nixon seems to be saying he doesn't need it anymore, since he's in the process of withdrawing troops. We're still here, though. I'm not a great believer in the theory that Congress cannot grant approval for military action short of declaring war. I've never seen that in the Constitution, but what does it mean when it grants approval and then withdraws it?

As ever,

Mike

SP4 Michael Ward

Fire Support Base Las Vegas

Republic of Vietnam

July 1, 1970

Dear Jane,

Doug Grayson, one of the other guys in FDC, got bitten by a scorpion yesterday. We were trying to plug up leaks in our bunker so that it will be watertight come the monsoon. To do that, we had to move a lot of sandbags. It was exhausting in this heat and also creepy. A lot of unsavory critters hang out under those things. The bite isn't as serious as it sounds, though. Scorpions in Vietnam are only about an inch and a half long, unlike the five-inch ones in the American Southwest. Being bitten by an American scorpion is like being bitten by a rattlesnake, while the bite of a Vietnamese one is more like a very bad bee sting. Regulations still required that Grayson be flown into Chu Lai for treatment. The creature looked like a miniature lobster. Jim Kallin grabbed our can of army-issue insecticide and sprayed it. The scorpion curled right up and died so fast that we were astonished. We couldn't believe that the stuff was that effective, so we read the contents off the can: DDT! I guess the army wasn't as impressed by Rachel Carson's *Silent Spring* as the Food and Drug Administration was.

I guess you're getting to the beach quite a bit now. Could you send me a picture of you by the ocean? While I love how you look in a bikini, I don't want the guys hanging all over me trying to look at it. Maybe one of those Victorian beach outfits like they show on the old postcards!

Love,

Mike

Patrick Ward

Sea Girt, New Jersey

July 2, 1970

Dear Mike,

The Yankees are out in Detroit, where they played the Tigers yesterday. It was billed as a big event, since it marked Denny McLain's return from his suspension for bookmaking. The game was not going too well for him after Jerry Kenney, Thurman Munson, and Bobby Murcer hit three home runs. McLain was pulled and replaced by Daryl Patterson, and the Tigers pulled ahead and won the game. McLain did receive a big standing ovation.

Your stereo arrived from Japan, and we put it in your room. Are you sure you know how to put it together? We hear everyone who comes home from Vietnam has a good stereo. Apparently, you will too now.

I was reading an article recently that discussed the unusual demographics of the current antiwar confrontations. Worldwide, most previous internal conflicts have been between the working class, pressing for change, and the elite, trying to maintain the status quo. Here in the United States, the working class, referred to as hard hats, are supporting the establishment, while most opposition comes from the so-called educated class. Just look at the recent standoff between the antiwar protesters in New York and the workers constructing the World Trade Center. I wonder what historians will say about that fifty years from now.

Your mother and I have both been wondering how you've made out with your hay fever in Vietnam. Does a tropical climate make it worse?

Affectionately,

Dad

SP4 Michael Ward

Fire Support Base Las Vegas

Republic of Vietnam

July 5, 1970

Dear Jane,

I just got your June 28 letter. It's a little after midnight now and it's quiet, so I have some time to respond. The inside of the bunker is still hot because of the sandbags. We do have an electric fan but no windows. None of us notice the smell anymore, but if you were to walk in here, you would probably fall over. As much as I miss you, this is not a place you would like to be.

When I was growing up, I also wondered what it was like for my parents in World War II. My father was away at sea for three years. My mother and her sister, whose husband was in the army, moved back with my grandmother. They must have felt their lives had taken a radical detour. I always pictured it as some kind of romantic challenge, but I could never imagine how that really felt. While everyone's experiences are different, at least it seems like those things are no longer a mystery now for either of us. They may have been married, but their family plans were sure put on hold. Now we know why there's a baby boom generation.

You're right, living through a war makes you look at everything from a whole different vantage point, but it's just so different for us than it was for them. My mother and her family had the support and respect of everyone around them. While their husbands were at war, she and her sister were looked on as patriots in their own right. How much of that do you get? Thank God for the auto mechanic. God bless that broken key! What else do we have? It was never my intent to leave you to face this type of situation on your own. I am sorry that's what I ended up doing.

You mentioned occupied World War II France. The French were divided like we are now. Many cooperated with the German occupation; others fought against it. Our war protesters probably think they're just like the resistance because they're confronting the government in power. The fact that this government was elected by our own people and isn't the result of a conquest by foreigners might escape them, but they could be sincere, even if they're missing the point of it all. We need to get the country back together, but what will it take? A victory here? A defeat? I hope not.

Love,

Mike

SP4 Michael Ward

Fire Support Base Las Vegas

Republic of Vietnam

July 6, 1970

Dear Sean,

It looks like my semi-safe existence on an established firebase is coming to an end. We just got word that we're going on a jump soon. That has nothing to do with jumping out of anything. What it does mean is we have to move to a temporary location with some of our guns, since the infantry will be operating beyond the range of the ones at this base. Most of the other guys have done this before and are telling me not to worry, but this one is going to be tougher than usual. The area where we're going is far west of here and deep in the jungle. Last year, another artillery battery and infantry battalion tried to operate in that area. The NVA drove off the battery, which forced the infantry to pull out. It couldn't operate without artillery support. Now the brass wants us to give it a try.

The prospect of this thing has us all a little jittery It will be the first time we're actually trying to gain ground here. We've fired a lot of missions from Las Vegas, but those were just to support infantry operating in the Rocket Pocket. Their main objective was to keep enemy units far enough away from Chu Lai that they wouldn't be able to fire rockets at the American base there. You can't win a war that way. Gen. Patton once said that he didn't want any of his units holding their position; that was for the enemy to do while he moved forward. Well anyway, that's what we're doing now.

I still don't have a clear picture of what's happening here. From everything I can see, most of the Vietnamese people are genuinely glad to have the Americans around but are unwilling to take any chances themselves. Dislike of the NVA and Viet Cong seems to be intense, yet those forces have no trouble whatsoever obtaining help and shelter from the villagers. The people's attitude appears to be one of helplessness. They wish we could do more, but if we can't, they'll make their own arrangements.

As ever,

Mike

Chapter 3
THE JUNGLE

Jane O'Brien

Spring Lake, New Jersey

July 7, 1970

Dear Michael,

Saturday was the Fourth of July. There wasn't much in the way of fireworks, not with the weather we were having. I can't imagine your type of fireworks ever getting rained out, not that you would consider explosions a form of celebration, anyway. What do artillerymen do to celebrate Independence Day?

By the way, you don't wear underwear! How about after you get home? ☺ If I tried to go to school without a bra, I'd probably be fired.

Did you remember that this is the third anniversary of our first date? I did. I guess I have to think about something other than where we are now! I recall how nervous I was after first meeting you at the hospital picnic. I was afraid you were never going to call me. You seemed so shy, I thought maybe I should call you first. But you did call, even if it was an unusual first date. Never mind! We did start going to the beach together then, and we could sometimes get a beer at one of the group rental parties. Then Eddie, my flame from down in Washington, decided it was time to visit. Oh, dear! It's not like we were ever really a hot item. Who knows what he thought, but he never called again after I got back down to Trinity. Good thing! I have no idea what he's doing now. I doubt he's in Vietnam, but I'd much rather be with you anyway. If only I were!

Love,

Jane

Mrs. Patrick Ward

Sea Girt, New Jersey

July 7, 1970

Michael dear,

I was washing the sand off my feet at about four o'clock yesterday when all the sirens and horns started to blow so hard I thought the Martians had landed. It was a Monmouth County general alarm for firemen and police to help quell a riot—burning, etc.—in Asbury Park. I haven't heard anything yet this morning, but I'm sure there will be a lot of news reports. It's hard to believe that something like that could happen down here. I am going to St. Mark's card party at the Monmouth Hotel this afternoon, and most likely some of the other ladies will have more information.

When you first went to Vietnam, people were telling us not to worry, that the time would just fly by and you would be home again. Well, it sure doesn't seem to be flying for me, and I doubt it is for you either, but it is passing as it must.

There is a tiny little rabbit living in our backyard here. He seems to love the fact that he can eat the lettuce right out of your father's garden. He won't budge, either, even if Dad is out there. He seems to feel the garden is his and your father is the intruder.

Lots of love,

Mom

SP4 Michael Ward

Fire Support Base Las Vegas

Republic of Vietnam

July 8, 1970

Dear Mom & Dad,

You had asked about how many people we have here at Las Vegas. The only regular units are the two artillery batteries. Our 105mm battery has about eighty men, and the 155mm battery has about a hundred. There is usually an infantry platoon staying here, which gives us another thirty. When they are here, they man the guard posts on the perimeter. We used to have two engineer companies, but they've been pulled out. There's an ARVN (Army of the Republic of Vietnam) platoon staying in their area now. They're busy tearing down buildings and should leave when they're finished.

We do have a laundry shop here on the firebase called Lee Lee's Laundry Shop. The Vietnamese woman who runs it has preprinted tickets that say "YOU WILL BE PLEASED OF OUR JOB." The items are listed in both English and Vietnamese. Trousers are "quan tran"; coats are "ao tran." In any event, we don't have to wash them ourselves.

I understand the Defense Department issued a statement June 29 denying it was assigning college graduate soldiers to jobs below their qualifications. While my rank may not be very high, I can't say that my job isn't challenging. I haven't done this much plane geometry since high school, and there's even some trigonometry thrown in. Living conditions may not be wonderful, but I do feel my work is important.

Did they have the usual Fourth of July barbecue at the golf club this year? Please let me know how it went. I enjoy reading about nice meals. While the food here is nutritious, it is very bland. Sometimes all I can think about is a plate of lasagna with a glass of Chianti.

Love,

Mike

SP4 Michael Ward

Fire Support Base Las Vegas

Republic of Vietnam

July 9, 1970

Dear Jane,

It's Thursday about four o'clock in the morning. Nothing is happening. While in some ways that's a good thing, it does make me miss you more since I have nothing else to focus my attention on. When something does happen, we don't get any warning. One second, we're lethargic; the next, we're hyper. Even when we're reading, our attention is always on the radio. One cackle from it can shatter our composure and turn us into assiduous robots.

While attacks on our firebase are relatively infrequent, the infantry night defensive positions are always at risk. Since those units are somewhat small and never know how large the attacking unit is, they need our artillery fire to push back the attackers. It's nerve-wracking because the opposing sides are usually a couple of miles from us but right on top of each other. There's no way for us to shoot without coming close to our own people.

It's not so bad when the attackers are to the left

or the right of the infantry from our perspective. We should be able to point the guns in the right direction. The real problem is when they are on a direct line either between us and our own infantry or on the other side of our infantry from us. Even if all our settings and calculations are correct, the distance a projectile travels can be affected by how long the shell has sat out in the sun or how much dampness it has been exposed to.

Range can be tricky. To reduce the risk in those situations, we always fire a white phosphorous round first and time it so it explodes fifty meters above the ground. If it explodes over the correct target, the forward observer will say, "Repeat H E on the deck," which means to put the next round on the ground in the same location, directly under the previous one, and make it a high-explosive round instead of a white phosphorous one. Often we find that the enemy attack ceases as soon as the first white phosphorous round goes off over their heads. They know what's coming next.

One of my friends here, Andy Winberry, has been telling me about salmon fishing. He's from Oregon, and it's big there. He likes to fly fish for salmon using waders and has won a few fishing contests. Salmon is the one thing he misses most about our food here. Fat chance he'll ever get that from the army!

I hope our enlightened state legislators' thoughts about the 179-year-old law are the same as yours and mine. I can't picture you and me as being the modern equivalent of Bonnie and Clyde, but I'd be willing to go that route if that's what it took.

Back to my reading now until breakfast. I'm working on *The Two Towers,* the second part of *The Lord of the Rings* by J. R. R. Tolkien.

Love,

Mike

SP4 Michael Ward

LZ Hurrah

Republic of Vietnam

July 11, 1970

Dear Mom & Dad,

We're out on a jump now west of Firebase Las Vegas. We're supposed to do this whenever the infantry operates beyond the range of the guns there. We brought four of our 105mm howitzers with us and left two at FSB Las Vegas. Our position is in a clearing on a hilltop. The surrounding area is all jungle. It's very secure here. We have a lot of infantry around the hill providing protection. Our FDC operates out of a large metal container that was brought by helicopter. Believe it or not, we are using a jeep to generate electricity. The radios and FADAC are hooked up to that. We sleep behind the FDC under corrugated culvert halves that are supported on signposts running from the FDC container to a ridge about five feet away. The culvert halves are covered with sandbags, so we have a roof over our heads, if no walls on two sides.

We can see far from here. The area is beautiful. It reminds me of Kipling's *The Jungle Book,* which was set in South Asia. We are so high up that when we shoot artillery, we can see the projectiles traveling through the air to their target. I've sent film to Kodak to be developed. The finished pictures will be sent to you, so you'll be able to see some of what it looks like. One of the photos will show a man with both his fists raised in the air talking to a small group of soldiers. That is Capt. Berlen giving instructions to the forward observers. He always makes his points dramatically.

We are eating C rations since there are no cooking facilities here. They are good and nutritious, if a little repetitive, and we can heat them up with heating tabs. It's funny how we take the empty can from our last meal, put several holes in the side, put the heating tab in, light it, and put the new full can on top. It's like having a miniature stove. They do bring out a water trailer every day by helicopter.

Did I really read the news correctly that the Louisiana state legislature refused to remove racial labels from blood donations and that one of the representatives said he would rather see his family members die than have them receive blood from a black person? I wonder if those family members would agree. He didn't make any such offer with his own life. He'd have a hard time over here!

Love,

Mike

Jane O'Brien

Spring Lake, New Jersey

July 12, 1970

Dear Michael,

Do you believe that someone is making midi skirts for men now? Rebecca Welles, the designer, says men will wear them on the golf course or around the pool. Would you like me to get you one for your birthday? I'll buy it if you let me take a picture of you. Do you have any Scottish blood?

Newark has its first Negro mayor. It's about time. His name is Kenneth Gibson, and he's an engineer. It will probably be some time before we see anything like that in Jersey City. Our population base is too diverse. The Newark riots may be a thing of the past, but look at what's happened in Asbury Park! The people I talk to around here are finding this much more shocking. Asbury Park, a beach resort with a boardwalk, shopping, and luxury hotels! They say when the race riots first started several years ago, President Johnson was really shaken by it. He felt he had done more for civil rights than any prior president. Well, it certainly wasn't his only surprise. Just look at where you are right now.

As the summer moves along, I have been to a few more of the bars: Jimmy Byrne's, the Keynote and the Parker House, just with the girls. There seems to be a rule that we're not allowed to buy ourselves drinks. Guys keep offering to get them for me. I say no most of the time. Otherwise, I'd be very drunk. Maybe that's what they want. The ones that ask are not the problem, though. It's the creeps who try to push drinks into your hand, usually nothing you'd ever order, that really turn me off. Do you even know what a slow gin fizz is?

I'm reading a lot, mostly on the beach if it's not raining. I've already read most of the bestsellers that interest me: *Love Story, The French Lieutenant's Woman, The Godfather,* etc., so now I'm on to the classics I never reached before. I finished *The House of the Seven Gables* and have started *The Scarlet Letter.* Although I was somewhat familiar with the theme of the story, I never realized that the reason they had to come up with such a unique punishment for Hester was that they could not prove her husband was still alive and, without that, they technically could not prove adultery. If they could, she would have been hanged. I'm not sure that the Massachusetts courts are getting any better. They recently sentenced a doctor to three months in jail for giving contraceptive foam to an "unmarried Boston University coed." The law prohibiting that has since been declared unconstitutional.

I'm still missing you terribly. Keep your head down.

Love,

Jane

SP4 Michael Ward

LZ Hurrah

Republic of Vietnam

July 13, 1970

Dear Sean,

This is the place I told you about. It's called LZ (Landing Zone) Hurrah. The NVA didn't make much of an effort to stop us from getting here, but we could certainly tell that the last unit left in a hurry. There was US Army debris everywhere. We have four of our guns with us plus an infantry mortar platoon. The sleeping arrangements are rough. We're like a pack of wolves lying on the ground under culvert halves behind the FDC. Our sanitation isn't much better, as there are no latrines, not even our half fifty-gallon drums.

We arrived on a large Chinook helicopter with a howitzer slung underneath. Each of us had to carry an artillery round on our shoulder so we could load the gun right away if we landed "hot." That means under enemy fire, but it didn't happen. We wear our helmets and flak jackets all the time here, but not shirts.

Fortunately, we can wash at the water trailer—at least we could until it got hit by a mortar, which brings up another story.

It was dark and very foggy, so was difficult getting the medevac helicopter in for the wounded. I was talking to the pilot on the radio from inside our temporary FDC, which is more like a modified shipping container. I realized I needed to get outside so I could hear better. I grabbed a PRC-25 portable backpack radio and headed out there. (PRC stands for portable radio communicator, but everyone calls it a "prick.") It was so foggy and dark we couldn't see the helicopter but we could hear it, and when it was directly overhead, we could feel the downdraft from its rotary blades. I told the pilot to come straight down. The copter was only six feet off the ground when we could finally see its landing struts below the fog line. From there on, everything went fine.

I read that vandals in Chicago have destroyed a monument to Medal of Honor winner Milton Olive, a black soldier who threw himself on a live grenade to save fellow soldiers. Of course, according to Mayor Lindsay, the "real heroes" are those living with the consequences of fleeing to Canada. A Catholic chaplain came and said Mass in the mortar pit yesterday. We sat on the sandbags around him. It felt more spiritual than being inside the walls of a church.

As ever,

Mike

Mrs. Patrick Ward

Sea Girt, New Jersey

July 14, 1970

Michael dear,

♬ *Allons enfants de la patrie* ♬ and all that—Happy Bastille Day. It is not yet ten o'clock, and I've taken a ride to the beach to see the sun on the ocean and watch the tennis players. Did I tell you about the phrase in the *Times* crosswords puzzle that had us stumped for a while? "Relax at sea." All of a sudden, it came to me: "Splice the main brace." Imagine forgetting that after all the times we've heard it used to announce cocktail hour!

More of your stereo parts arrived from Japan and are in your room. We did not unpack them. It's fortunate we were back in the city when the package came. The delivery man told us he served in Vietnam in the infantry as a machine gunner.

William Birenbaum, the president of Staten Island Community College, gave a speech at Fort Dix the other day where he said the Vietnam veteran is the most neglected veteran in American history. You don't say! Johnny Cash recently commented, "I hope they bring all the men from Vietnam home soon. Remember I said men, not boys. There are no boys in Vietnam." I see that the Chinese communists have finally released Bishop Walsh, but why did they hold him in prison for twelve years in the first place?

Joan O'Mara's wedding was Saturday. It was lovely. All the neighbors from our block were there, and they were all asking for you. We left early to drive down here.

Lots of love,

Mom

Patrick Ward

Jersey City, New Jersey

July 14, 1970

Dear Mike,

Last weekend I took your car out and drove it around. It ran like a watch—no trouble at all. I wish my own were doing as well. As you know, it has head-light covers. Well, now they won't open. Just something else to go wrong.

The Law School Moot Court case this year was based on an actual appeal from a conviction for the unauthorized wearing of a distinctive part of an army uniform. Some demonstrators, wearing military uniforms, put on a show of supposed atrocities by GIs in front of a draft board to protest the war. They claimed that the conviction infringed on their rights of free speech and also that it came within the exception of the law: use of a uniform by an actor in a play "if the

portrayal does not tend to discredit that armed force."
The conviction was upheld in the actual case. Of
course, the Moot Court panel does not decide which
party should win the case, only which students make
the most effective arguments.

All his usual bluster notwithstanding, I was surprised to see Vice President Agnew publicly criticize
a Nixon appointee to the Commission on Campus
Unrest as "harebrained," especially since the president
had refused to rescind the appointment. It makes it
look like he's now targeting Nixon, despite the latter's
strong support of him.

Affectionately,

Dad

Jane O'Brien

Spring Lake, New Jersey

July 16, 1970

Dear Michael,

I hope you looked at the photo before starting
to read this letter. If not, stop reading and look at
the picture first. You said you wanted one of me at
the beach in Victorian bathing attire, so look what
you got—four of us. Beth Harahan, Ginny McLeod,
Angela Sestina, and me. It was Angela who found the
outfits in a costume shop in Manasquan. We bought
an old black-and-white postcard in the drugstore to

use as a model. We were quite the hit at the beach. We had no trouble getting someone to take the picture. There were more volunteers than there were of us. It was also no problem getting people in modern bathing suits to stay out of the way when the photo was snapped. It caused quite a sensation. Everyone talked about the fact that it was being sent to soldiers in Vietnam. They thought it was a very strange type of picture to send to our men in uniform! Maybe it is, but I don't care. It's the only fun thing I've done lately! Do you think we have what it takes to be pinups?

About the DDT, as much as I am a fan of Rachel Carson, if we were to make just one exception to the usual rule, it would be for scorpions! Don't go walking around in your bare feet.

Love,

Jane

SP4 Michael Ward

LZ Hurrah

Republic of Vietnam

July 18, 1970

Dear Sean,

The NVA have been keeping up the pressure on us here. Once it turns dark, the question isn't if we'll get attacked but when and from what direction. It's not just the North Vietnamese. There are Chinese regulars here as well, not something that gets much press. We are still making out much better than the last unit.

Two nights ago, I had to call in air support. We were receiving small arms and automatic weapons fire on our southeast perimeter, and there was more coming at us than going out. We have no barbed wire here and we're the only artillery in town, so Capt. Berlen told me to call for whatever help we could get. One very strange-looking plane showed up. It was propeller-driven and slow-flying, with a split tail. Bill Davis told me it was called a Shadow. The first thing it did was drop an enormous flare that seemed to turn night into day. Then it opened fire outside our perimeter with a mini-gun, which consists of six synchronized M-60 machine guns that fire so fast they don't sound like machine guns at all but rather like a loud hum. The tracer bullets made it look like a killer space ray. We had no further problems that night. Also, don't worry—as you can see, no matter what's happening, I spend most of my time talking on the radio.

Holding out,

Mike

SP4 Michael Ward

Fire Support Base Las Vegas

Republic of Vietnam

July 20, 1970

Dear Jane,

It's called a "*sloe* gin fizz" because it's made from sloe gin, which is purple and distilled from plums. You may or may not like it, but it's not something someone should procure for you unasked. It's not so universally loved that strangers should assume any young woman who tastes one will just adore it.

We just returned from what we call a jump, meaning we fly by helicopter (Chinook) with a howitzer slung underneath to set up a temporary firebase when the infantry goes beyond the normal range of our guns. Although it's not as secure as a permanent firebase since we have no barbed wire, we did have a lot of infantry with us, and it was a lot safer than walking through the jungle and stepping on land mines. We ate C rations most of the time since there was no mess hall, but we usually got fresh, cooked eggs in the morning, especially after one incident. Our original cook was wounded when the water trailer got hit by a mortar. One of the guys in FDC, Edwin Smart, is a black professional piano player from San Diego. He's also an excellent cook and volunteered to fill in for the wounded cook. From that point on, FDC always seemed to get the first allocation of fresh eggs.

I'm not sure it's any worse here than in Belfast right now. Whole neighborhoods there are being evacuated, and it's not even clear which side the British troops are fighting. For as long as we've been tied up in Vietnam, I fear Ireland will take considerably longer. Even Asbury Park is a problem. I wonder what effect that is having on the Johnny Mathis concert at Convention Hall?

Now I understand President Nixon has ordered the creation of a Vice Presidential Service Badge for military personnel assigned to the vice president. They certainly deserve something just for having to listen to him.

Love,

Mike

Mrs. Patrick Ward

Sea Girt, New Jersey

July 20, 1970

Michael dear,

Today is quite lovely. It was a little foggy this morning, but it's nice and clear now. I might go down to the beach once the sun is past its peak. You know how my skin is.

We got your letter about your new "Hurrah" location. It does not sound very peachy. I hope they don't keep you there too long. If it really is like Kipling's *The Jungle Book,* then keep an eye out for all sorts of animals and snakes. As if the Viet Cong were not enough!

Your father and I had dinner at the golf club Thursday. Friday and Saturday can be too crowded for us in the summer. The Brennans were there and had a guest with them, Meg Brennan's cousin. He's retired from the army, a colonel or general or something. He served two tours of duty in Vietnam and was telling us how important it is that President Nixon accomplish something at the Paris peace talks. He said our original strategy there was not working and we need to try a different approach. A negotiated settlement would be best.

A negotiated settlement! Best? What would really be best is to stop playing around with one inept scheme after another and just bring you all home. What makes them think any new brainchild will work better than the last?

Lots of love,

Mom

SP4 Michael Ward

Fire Support Base Las Vegas

Republic of Vietnam

July 21, 1970

Dear Mom & Dad,

We're back at Firebase Las Vegas now. While it's certainly not luxurious here, it's nice to have something that vaguely resembles a bed, not to mention a usable latrine. The men who stayed here with the other two guns while we were gone were real happy to see us come back. While we were away with the infantry, they felt the base was too undermanned to be secure. That's no longer a worry, and we're back seeing movies. Last night was *John and Mary* with Dustin Hoffman and Mia Farrow.

Well, some type of prisoner exchange is going through between the United States and North Vietnam. It's been blocked for the past two years because North Vietnam has denied that we have any of their soldiers to exchange. According to them, they have no troops in South Vietnam at all. Apparently, some deal was worked out with Admiral McCain, the US Pacific commander, for the North Vietnamese to take them back without admitting that they're theirs!

We have a new fire direction officer, Lt. David Fitzsimmons, a graduate of the ROTC program at Xavier University in Cincinnati. He's married, and his wife is expecting a baby. She's living in Cleveland. He's taking the place of Lt. Barnes, who left to go home today, back to Connecticut. He's the third one to leave from FDC since I got here. This is so different from World War II, when servicemen went and came back with the same guys. By the time I leave here, there will be no one left from when I arrived. It's no wonder people who have been here more than six months are treated like old sages. Will you mind if I'm an old sage when I come back?

Love,

Mike

SP4 Michael Ward

Fire Support Base Las Vegas

Republic of Vietnam

July 22, 1970

Dear Sean,

I don't get it. I just don't get it. We venture forth from our not-completely-safe firebase to a not-at-all-safe hilltop surrounded by jungle. We manage to hold it and complete our mission, something the last unit couldn't do. Then what happens? Nothing! We come back. To top it all off, Gen. Westmoreland is now saying that no American military leaders ever believed a military victory was possible in Vietnam "in the classical sense"! What is that supposed to mean? Are we fighting a war, or are we just going on some weird form of field exercise where people still get killed or maimed? This is not at all what I pictured this war to be like. Our whole "successful" operation didn't add one square inch of territory to South Vietnamese government control.

They lifted three stretchers onto that medevac helicopter I talked down. The soldier on at least one of them is going home minus a leg, and that doesn't even take into account the casualties suffered by the infantry units in the jungle we were supporting. They suffered serious casualties, too, including some killed. What did this accomplish? Why do I feel like

I'm doing my part? I go where they send me, but the overall scheme we're all following is more like a merry-go-round than a cavalry charge. Any real objective we could hope to obtain is sitting somewhere outside the carousel!

By the way, I bought the damn dogs myself. I walked to the village on Route 1 and got two puppies for five dollars. While I was there, I saw one of the kids Jim and I encountered next to the dirt road last month. I hope the dogs aren't VC spies. I'll keep an eye on them to see if they're taking any notes.

Not quite as ever,

Mike

SP4 Michael Ward

Fire Support Base Las Vegas

Republic of Vietnam

July 24, 1970

Dear Jane,

Do you have what it takes to be pinups?! The picture you sent is now stuck on the wall in FDC, and I've never seen any other pinup get that much attention. The others are all centerfolds from *Playboy*. For the most part, the girls are wearing nothing, but the pictures still don't draw many comments. Everyone who comes into the bunker and sees your photo, though, says something like "What on earth?" It doesn't hurt either that you're all gorgeous! I started out by telling the guys that all the women in New Jersey wear those types of suits to the beach, that dress codes there are very strict. I don't think that did much for my credibility. Think I could persuade you to wear that suit one more time next summer when I'm there so I can see you in it firsthand? If it's difficult to put on, I can help you with it!

As far as walking around in my bare feet, do you think I'm crazy? Even when we're in the shower, we wear sandals. The Vietnamese make them from old tires, probably from US military vehicles. The soles are cut out from the tread, and the straps are from other parts.

Love,

Mike

Mrs. Patrick Ward

Sea Girt, New Jersey

July 24, 1970

Michael dear,

The summer is moving fast—goody! It's not an unpleasant summer, but I just want you home. The weather has cleared nicely, and both the beach and the water are beautiful. Your Uncle Bill and Aunt Peggy were down with their young ones Wednesday. While they were enjoying the ocean, Bernadette and

I went over to Hinck's and got a cooked turkey with beans and salad. We ate at picnic tables in the backyard, and everyone was in good spirits. The enclosed photographs show all that. The one that has no people in it shows the baby rabbit. You may not be able to make him out without a magnifying glass, but he is under the bush. He wasn't about to leave, no matter how many people were there. I've never seen a bunny so possessive.

I ran into Monsignor Murphy the other day. As you know, he lives in Washington and works for the Catholic Hospital Association. He is heading for Vietnam soon to inspect the Catholic hospitals there. It's unlikely he will be anywhere near you. There appears to be a lot of concern about how those hospitals would make out if there were a North Vietnamese takeover. Catholic facilities do not tend to thrive under communist governments.

Lots of love,

Mom

Patrick Ward

Sea Girt, New Jersey

July 25, 1970

Dear Mike,

After twenty-two weeks, the Hudson County Black Panther trial ended in a mistrial. It's a shame.

With all the testimony and evidence already presented, a juror had a heart attack while the jury was deliberating. Doctors examined her and said she could not go on. Now it will have to be done all over again.

Today is Saturday but it's very stormy, so it won't be a beach day. For me, it won't be a golf day. I have a lot of reading to do for work, so maybe it's better this way. The Yankees are playing out in Oakland today. I may watch that for a while.

I imagine you're back from your operation by now. How hard is it to move those guns by helicopter? They must be heavy. At least when you're on a maneuver like that, everyone has to stay on his toes. No one's likely to slough off in that kind of environment. I'm sure the living conditions are not very good, but at least it's only short term. One of the advantages of being in the navy was that I had the same bunk for three years.

Affectionately,

Dad

Jane O'Brien

Spring Lake, New Jersey

July 26, 1970

Dear Michael,

The weather is beautiful today, so I'm going down to the beach with my book of the week, *Dracula* by

Bram Stoker. As all I get to do on the beach anymore is read, I may as well try an Irish classic!

Speaking of literature, what's going on with Edgar Smith? Why is he getting literary recognition from an international writers association that champions authors imprisoned for political reasons? He's no political prisoner. He was convicted of the very brutal murder of a high school cheerleader. That conviction is still standing, despite many appeals. The association is telling everyone that the only requirement for this honor is the publication of works of literary quality. Why do I feel that's not what's really happening? William F. Buckley Jr. has been championing Smith's cause for years. Is the association trying to suggest he's innocent, or does it seriously mean that it would honor a writer regardless of whatever heinous things he may have done? I have trouble accepting the latter.

Love,

Jane

Jane O'Brien

Spring Lake, New Jersey

July 27, 1970

What do you mean your cook was wounded when the water trailer got hit by a mortar? What happened to attacks on your base being infrequent and feeling like you were in a prison rather than an armed camp, and what were you doing someplace with no barbed wire fencing? More important than that, why did you feel you had to bury that comment somewhere after a discussion about a slow or sloe or whatever gin fizz? Michael, that's like rambling on about the weather for a page before telling someone that a mutual friend has died.

You know what? If you're not going to tell me the truth, then just don't bother writing.

Jane

Chapter 4
ESTRANGEMENT

Mrs. Patrick Ward

Sea Girt, New Jersey

July 28, 1970

Michael dear,

Aunt Anne died at four thirty this afternoon. It was all very peaceful. The afternoon and evening have been busy with calls and such, so I'm rushing. I don't know anything about arrangements yet. We'll miss her. As sick and out of it that she was most of the time, she always wanted to know when you were coming home. As you can imagine, this letter has to be short!

Lots of love,

Mom

Mrs. Patrick Ward

Sea Girt, New Jersey

July 31, 1970

Michael dear,

Anne's funeral was this morning at St. Mark's. It was done very beautifully with Monsignor Murphy presiding at the concelebrated Mass. There were flowers from us with all four of our names. Uncle Bob and Bernadette had a catered reception back at the house afterwards. Bob commented that it would have been a good party if Anne had been there.

There was one strange thing, however. While we were all at the Mass, a young man came to the house and told the caterer he was there to pick up Mrs. Clarke's car, that he was the mechanic who'd been called. The caterer refused to give him the keys, and the man got a little nasty but finally left. Of course, no one had called a mechanic. The police told Bob that this is a new scam, that some people read the death notices in the newspaper, go to the homes during the funeral services, and try to con whoever's there into giving them the keys to the dead person's car. Can you believe that?

I don't mean to pry too much, but is something not right with Jane? She came to the funeral home during the wake, signed the book, and left without speaking to anybody. Even her handwriting in the book looked very shaky. It's very strange.

Lots of love,

Mom

SP4 Michael Ward

Fire Support Base Las Vegas

Republic of Vietnam

August 1, 1970

Dear Mom & Dad,

According to Secretary of Defense Laird, casualties in Vietnam are at their lowest level since 1966 and the fiscal cost of the war has now been cut in half. Those things may be good in and of themselves, but I don't know what they're leading up to. How is this all going to end?

On a less somber note, I see Aristotle Onassis is giving Jackie the "world's best yacht" for her birthday. Apparently, she's getting congratulations from everyone from her former brother-in-law, Ted Kennedy, to Richard Burton and Elizabeth Taylor.

It's been very hot here lately, but there hasn't been a whole lot of activity. Maybe Laird is right. We had pork chops for lunch, and I got a haircut from the Vietnamese barber set up over at the other battery. Our level of physical activity here is kind of erratic. We're either knocking ourselves out filling and moving sandbags in the heat or, more often, just sticking pins in charts and moving slide rules. None of us seem to put on any weight, though.

I do think a lot about what it would be like to be home now, not just about the beach and the beach bars but wearing real clothes that stay dry. Simply thinking about sitting in a chair and reading, wearing shoes and socks and slacks and a shirt and underwear, is a comforting feeling. This will all pass, and I know I will look back on this someday as one of the more interesting times in my life, but right now I look forward to looking back.

Love,

Mike

SP4 Michael Ward

Fire Support Base Las Vegas

Republic of Vietnam

August 4, 1970

Dear Jane,

Hold the presses! The California State Legislature has just passed a bill allowing cocktail lounges to be called "saloons" rather than "taverns." Does that mean customers will have to wear cowboy hats and carry six-guns to stand at the bar? You, of course, could always wear one of those dance hall dresses like Miss Kitty on *Gunsmoke.*

We're not too busy. I guess the NVA are napping for a while. Kind of them to let me have time to write you a letter. They can really be very considerate occasionally. I've been reading the paper. The Charles Manson (Tate-LaBianca) murder trial is big news even here. It's hard to imagine the hold Manson would have had to have on his followers to get them to do those grisly killings. His attorney appears to be following the new radical defense practice of disrupting the proceedings instead of presenting a real defense. Whatever benefit defendants may derive from that practice in a trial with quasi-political overtones, I don't see it working where the charge is an out-and-out thrill killing.

Damon Williams left yesterday to go home to Georgia. Everyone was sorry to see him go (except him, of course). He was a big, good-natured guy with about as large a mustache as the army would allow and then some. I don't think he'll be looking for any martinis, though. Even if it weren't for his religious position, no one would think well of that libation if his only taste of one had come from a canteen rather than a cocktail glass with a lemon twist.

Love,

Mike

SP4 Michael Ward

Fire Support Base Las Vegas

Republic of Vietnam

August 5, 1970

Dear Mom & Dad,

I was sorry to hear about Aunt Anne, although it was not unexpected. It was time for her suffering to end. I will say a prayer for her and write to Uncle Bob and Bernadette. It's a busy time of day here working up the firing data for the infantry NDPs and their defensive targets, so I can't take long now.

Love,

Mike

SP4 Michael Ward

Fire Support Base Las Vegas

Republic of Vietnam

August 5, 1970

Dear Jane,

I just got your letter from July 27. I'm sorry. I was just trying to keep you from worrying more. You wrote me that you wake up every morning wondering if you'll get bad news. I didn't want to aggravate that. Even if you look at my last letter to Sean (I'll tell him to show you whatever you want), you'll see that I'm still just talking on the radio, no matter what happens.

I won't trouble you with anything else now, but please get back to me.

Love,

Mike

SP4 Michael Ward

Fire Support Base Las Vegas

Republic of Vietnam

August 6, 1970

Dear Sean,

We are back in our luxurious bunker now at Firebase Las Vegas. The rats were happy to see us return. Now there's more food for them to steal.

Jane and I have been writing. I'm going to have to go into more detail in my letters to her. I'll tell her she can look at my letters to you too, so please show her whatever. I guess there's stuff she should know, even if she wouldn't be interested in how to set up a time on target.

As ever,

Mike

SP4 Michael Ward

Fire Support Base Las Vegas

Republic of Vietnam

August 6, 1970

Dear Uncle Bob and Bernadette,

Although I know it was not unexpected, I was deeply saddened to hear about Aunt Anne's death.

May perpetual light shine upon her! I will pray for her and for you.

Life here has been quiet for the past couple of weeks. We were out in the field for a while in July but are back at our regular base now. Most of our work here involves plotting defensive targets to protect our infantry units. Charlie Battery (that's us) generally supports three infantry companies in the bush at any given time. Every night we have to mark their positions on charts and prepare a defense for them if they get attacked. It's very exacting and intensive work with no room for error.

I look forward to being on the beach with you next summer.

Love,

Mike

Mrs. Patrick Ward

Sea Girt, New Jersey

August 6, 1970

Michael dear,

Mrs. Boyd is down for the week and is staying at the Hewitt Wellington. We are having her over for dinner on Saturday and have invited three other couples. Bob and Bernadette are coming. They need to get out more now. I think your father is going to cook steaks out on the charcoal grill if the weather holds up.

What I thought was a flash of good news turned into a disappointment. Congressman MacGregor of Minnesota had said that by next May there would be no US ground forces left in Vietnam. That sounded wonderful. Then the Nixon administration clarified that there will still be American infantry and artillery there but that they will be used solely to protect American facilities. All ground combat operations, however, will pass to the South Vietnamese.

One of the candidates for New York State attorney general has suggested that the solution to New York's air pollution problem is to sue the New Jersey factories he says are producing it. Well then, how come their problems develop only when the air is stagnant and go away when the wind picks up? If what he says were true, it would be just the opposite.

Mayor Lindsay seems to be trying to mend fences. He gave a big party yesterday at Gracie Mansion for wounded Vietnam veterans. All three of his daughters were there and danced with the servicemen. Lindsay denied this had anything to do with his prior comments. One might question his veracity on that point, but at least he's going in the right direction.

Lots of love,

Mom

Jane O'Brien

Spring Lake, New Jersey

August 7, 1970

Dear Michael,

I cried myself to sleep the night I got your letter about the cook and the mortar, and not for his
sake. It really can't go on like this. If we were married
and you were diagnosed with a serious illness, whom
would you tell first, Sean or me? Maybe we can start
over, but only if I'm at the center of your inner circle
As unhappy as I am that you are in Vietnam, as long
as you're there, I want you to think of me as standing beside you. Please, please, please don't keep things
from me.

While I was at the beach today with Beth and
Angela, we were discussing Dr. Edgar Berman's
resignation from the Democratic National Committee's policy council. It was provoked by his comments
that women are completely unfit to be anything like
president of the United States. He even suggested that
doctors who think otherwise don't know enough about
premenstrual tension and should go back to medical
school. Congresswoman Patsy Mink of Hawaii had
been pushing for his resignation. Supposedly, he had
asked her what might happen if a woman in meno-
pause had to deal with the Bay of Pigs or the Cuban
Missile Crisis. She got former Vice President Humphrey to call Berman, but that's not why he resigned,
or so he says. He claims it was because his wife and his
dog were getting "bored" with all the furor.

"Bored!" Is that what he really thinks they were? Even the pooch seems to be more on the ball than he is, but that's not why I'm bringing this up. You and Dr. Berman seem to suffer from a similar problem. Why do you think Sean can handle the truth better than I can? What is really going on over there? One minute you're on a well-protected firebase, the next you're sleeping on the ground God knows where. Just tell me what's really happening. I promise I won't behave like Dr. Berman says I should, no matter what time of the month it is.

On a different topic, I read that the sharp reduction in American forces has created another serious problem in Vietnam, runaway unemployment for prostitutes. So many of them are being forced out of work and are returning to their homes that the small hamlets are having trouble coping with them all. Is it really that big an industry there?

Love,

Jane

SP4 Michael Ward

Fire Support Base Las Vegas

Republic of Vietnam

August 7, 1970

Dear Mom & Dad,

I don't think I've told you about the money we

have here. We're not allowed to carry American currency. I think the reason has something to do with the black market. Instead, we're issued what are called military payment certificates or MPCs for short. There are no coins, so even nickels are paper. In theory only US servicemen are allowed to spend them, but Vietnamese will take them quite readily. Obviously, someone either accepts MPCs from them or changes them into other currency for them. Periodically, we're told to turn in all our MPC's and we're issued new ones of different design. The old ones then become worthless. The idea is that anyone other than US military personnel who has them will get stuck with the old, worthless certificates. For some reason, the whole idea doesn't impress me.

I was reading a news article on President Thieu's speech Friday. He says that after a cease-fire, he would be willing to have a national election in which the Viet Cong would be entitled to participate. He said he does not want a "leopard skin" Vietnam with patches of Viet Cong-controlled areas cut out from the rest of the country. He seems confident that the communists could not win a nationwide election and wants to avoid strictly regional ones. This is consistent with my impression that the majority of the people here do not want communist rule. The country was partitioned for a reason, with the north opting for communism and the south opting out of it. You would think if North Vietnam really believed the majority of the people in

South Vietnam were in favor of a communist takeover, it would welcome such an election.

All of that is fine and dandy, but there's not going to be any election. Between what Gen. Westmoreland is now saying and what's obvious to us all here, despite all our effort, suffering, and heartbreak, we're accomplishing absolutely nothing. You can't win a war by constantly capturing the same ground over and over again and giving it back over and over again. Our soldiers are good and loyal and devoted, no matter what some people at home think. Make no mistake, even the most stouthearted among us will not persevere in support of a strategy that repeatedly discards the fruits of every sacrifice we make.

I'm sorry. I don't want to sound depressed. I still feel my work is important. It's what keeps a lot of people alive, and if it's detrimental to others, well, they're the aggressors. They're the ones who want to take over someone else's country. We may not be able to stop them, but we can limit the human suffering they cause.

Love,

Mike

SP4 Michael Ward

Fire Support Base Las Vegas

Republic of Vietnam

August 9, 1970

Dear Jane,

We had an attack here at this firebase last night. No one in our battery was killed or wounded, but there were casualties in the other battery. Some of their bunkers and their FDC got blown up. I was outside, but the only thing that came anywhere near me was a mortar round on the other side of the FDC bunker from me. I am going into a little more detail with Sean, with technical stuff that might not interest you, but you are welcome to look at it if you want.

Love,

Mike

SP4 Michael Ward

Fire Support Base Las Vegas

Republic of Vietnam

August 9, 1970

Dear Sean,

Our shift was on duty last night in the FDC when we heard a series of explosions at about eleven o'clock. Lt. Fitzsimmons called up the exec post to find out what was happening and was told that we appeared to be under attack by sappers who were inside our wire and had already blown up the FDC of the other battery. He told me to go up and guard the door to our bunker so the same thing wouldn't happen to us. During an attack, the guys on the off-duty shift are supposed to defend the FDC, but it would take them a minute or two to get their boots on, grab their weapons, flak jackets, and helmets and get out there, so I had to fill in the gap.

The door is at the top of stairs from underground. Even though it can be barred shut, it's safer during an attack to have it open with an armed guard there. Otherwise, it would be too easy to blow open. There's a three-sided barricade outside the door made of wooden ammunition boxes filled with dirt, so there's something to stand behind. Eddie Dolan, our generator operator who's been here a lot longer than I have, came over and pointed out bunkers to me that were on fire. Since the flames were coming from the inside, he said they had to be from satchel charges thrown into them rather than mortar fire.

We were standing outside the barrier when we felt a fierce rush of air over our heads, which made us dive back into the FDC entrance. I don't even remember hearing a blast, but a mortar had hit the ground on the other side of the bunker. With all the training we've had about mortar fire trying to catch people in the open after the satchel charges exploded, you'd think we'd know enough to stay under cover! What happened next was surreal. One of the defensive devices on our perimeter consists of fougasses, fifty-gallon drums filled with thickened gasoline (also called napalm) with a small explosive charge at the bottom of the drum. The drum is tipped at a forty-five-degree angle toward the outside. If the charge gets set off, it shoots burning fuel out in a wave-like fashion. We have a number of these fougasses on our perimeter, all of which went off at once during the mortar barrage, sending out an enormous, terrifying flaming wave that lit up the whole area like a movie set. At first we thought it must have been intentionally triggered in response to a ground attack, but we later learned one of the mortars had struck a fougasse, all of which are connected by an explosive daisy-chain cord, causing them to fire simultaneously.

One thing that surprised us was despite what we'd been taught during our in-country training in Chu Lai, the sappers cut the barbed wire rather than just pulling the coils apart and tying them back. They tied the wire closed with string before cutting it, probably on an earlier night. Then on the night of the attack, all they had to do was to cut the strings, which was much faster than having to cut the wire that night. The perimeter patrols have been alerted to check the wire during daylight in the future to see if any has been cut and tied together with string.

As ever,

Mike

Patrick Ward

Sea Girt, New Jersey

August 9, 1970

Dear Mike,

There was quite a to-do yesterday at Yankee Stadium. As part of Old-Timers Day, Casey Stengel's number 37 was retired. It now joins number 3, Babe Ruth; number 4, Lou Gehrig; number 5, Joe DiMaggio; and number 7, Mickey Mantle, in being unavailable to future players. Stengel commented that now that he had a retired number, he planned on dying in it.

I see that former Kennedy White House Aide O'Donnell recently claimed that President Kennedy had made plans to withdraw all US troops from Vietnam after the 1964 presidential election, which would have been carried out had he not been assassinated. Vice President Agnew responded by saying it was "bad taste" to write that a dead president would risk American lives for two years after the decision had already been made to withdraw from Vietnam. Leaving aside the veracity or lack thereof of the allegation, can't it be argued that Nixon is doing exactly that right now?

I just read that starting in October, First New Jersey Bank is going to have machines that dispense money directly to customers. I've never heard of anything like that before and can foresee all types of problems. Apparently, any person using a machine will have to insert a credit card for identification. I'm sure the crooks will find some way to pervert that. One would also think that the Uniform Commercial Code will have to be updated to cover transactions of this nature. If that's not done, how would the law treat a counterfeit card? Would it be treated as a forged negotiable instrument or check? Time will tell.

Affectionately,

Dad

SP4 Michael Ward

Fire Support Base Las Vegas

Republic of Vietnam

August 12, 1970

Dear Mom & Dad,

Breakfast today was a lot better than yesterday: eggs to order, bacon, French toast. Yesterday we had powdered eggs. (Yech!)

We had some excitement the other day. Our friendly local NVA decided to pay us an unannounced visit. Don't worry. Our dirty little bunker remained unscathed.

The mail service here has been terrible lately. Not only is it very delayed, but some of the letters are arriving damaged. At some point, I'll try to make a MARS telephone call to you. Those calls are done on an open radio circuit, so they are not private. The calls are picked up by volunteer radio operators in the US, who then reroute them over a telephone line. The call from Vietnam to the States still has to go over the radio, so you have to remember to say "over" when you finish speaking so the operators know to change the push-to-talk buttons to reverse the direction of the transmission.

It doesn't bother me that some people protest the war and want it ended, but I do have trouble fathoming what legitimate purpose is served by a mob of "yippies" forcing the closing of Disneyland. Their rationale eludes me.

Love,

Mike

Jane O'Brien

Spring Lake, New Jersey

August 12, 1970

Dear Michael,

I just got your August 5 letter and looked over your earlier ones to Sean, just the ones sent down here to the shore. The others are up north. I promised myself not to rant and rave. No, I don't need to know every detail of what happens. I don't care what type of airplanes you have flying around you or what type of machine guns they shoot. But I do want you to tell me when you're going someplace like where you went.

Michael, you knew about that jump and wrote to Sean about it a week before you even left, but you didn't write anything to me about it until two weeks later. You never told me what had happened to the last American army unit to go there. I couldn't even pray about it until after it was over.

Love,

Jane

Bernadette Clarke

Sea Girt, New Jersey

August 12, 1970

Dear Mike,

Thank you for your letter about my mother. We all feel sad, but things had just gotten to the point where she couldn't go on. Your prayers are most appreciated. Your parents were also a real help. It was wonderful having them so close during the summer.

Looking after Mom was all I've done this past year. Now I have to get back into the job market. Teaching jobs have become a lot harder to obtain with all the men getting into the field. Maybe I should just find a husband who doesn't mind getting bills from Lord & Taylor. I've been dating, but there are no wedding bells on the horizon. Now that I have a little break, I'm going to try to get back to the beach. This is the first summer where I haven't had a tan by this point.

Speaking of the beach, that freighter is still there

Everyone says there's a big squabble involving the Borough of Sea Girt, the Coast Guard, and the shipping company as to who should remove it.

As far as local news, there's a dispute now between the Burlington County prosecutor and the Medford public safety director. The ACLU is claiming that the Medford police are stopping cars carrying long-haired young people on their way to the Jersey Shore from Philadelphia. They're complaining they're being searched for no apparent reason. The prosecutor seems to be siding with the ACLU, but the public safety director responded that these stops have resulted in a lot of arrests.

Love,

Bernadette

Mrs. Patrick Ward

Sea Girt, New Jersey

August 13, 1970

Michael dear,

The holly trees are loaded with berries. I just remarked to Dad that they will bloom around Christmas time. Usually that makes me feel so good. This year that will have to wait until you get home.

Your father arranged a small birthday party for me at the golf club yesterday. It was a good thing to do. I have been a little stick in the mud lately, which is not like me at all. All of the gals wore pantsuits, which is certainly a change from the way things used to be, but they looked marvelous in them.

There's a new ordinance proposed in Ocean City that would forbid anyone on the boardwalk from "being a member of a group of six or more, if any member of the group is wearing or carrying garb not normally used as wearing apparel and that could conceal a weapon." You may not have guessed it, but all that mixed-up wordage is supposed to keep hippies off the boardwalk. Someone either has a wild imagination or just a good sense of humor.

Lots of love,

Mom

SP4 Michael Ward

Fire Support Base Las Vegas

Republic of Vietnam

August 14, 1970

Dear Jane,

I just got your August 7 letter. It's hard to know what to say. I'm not trying to deceive you, and I certainly don't share Dr. Berman's opinions, whatever you think. Most of what we have here is boredom and isolation. I'm afraid if I make too much of our few direct encounters with the enemy, it could cause you unjustified worry. I don't want to hide things from you, but mentioning one dicey situation could give a false impression. We're not the front line of defense here. We're more like second tier, not in the rear on a big base but not sleeping on the ground in the jungle every night, either. I wrote the way I did because I love you and don't want to sound like the type of warrior I'm not.

You asked about prostitutes. I'm sure it's a very big business in the cities. That's always going to happen when you ship hundreds of thousands of men but very few women someplace. Out here where we are, there's not very much of it. The villages aren't safe for any purpose, let alone one like that. I've heard one of the girls who works in the laundry on the firebase picks up some extra cash that way, but that's only one on the whole base. I wouldn't recommend those odds to anyone.

It's hard for people at home to understand how cut off we are here. The average soldier never gets to Saigon. At Danang, while you might pass through the airbase, it would be unusual to get into the actual city. The only large locations I have ever been in have been military bases like Bien Hoa, Long Binh, or Chu Lai. I don't have a clue what a Vietnamese restaurant is like and have never tasted a morsel of Vietnamese food. In some ways it's not like being in a foreign country at all.

We do occasionally get off the base. Sometimes we have to walk the two-mile dirt road from the firebase to Route 1, something we have to do very carefully and well armed. Once on Route 1, we can flag down a US Army truck. They'll pick up any American soldier who signals them. We do pass some villages on the way to Chu Lai, but we don't stop in them. The Vietnam you read about in the newspapers is, in most cases, not the one we get to see. It's nothing like visiting Japan or Hong Kong and staying in a hotel.

Love,

Mike

Jane O'Brien

Spring Lake, New Jersey

August 15, 1970

Dear Michael,

The Paris peace talks are looking worse and worse. Sure, North Vietnam has sent its chief delegate back there, but he's now saying the way to get things moving is for the United States to withdraw its troops "quickly and unconditionally." While I'm not really opposed to that since it might be the only real option left to us, it doesn't sound like anything I would call negotiation. Why are we even bothering talking with them? Is it just to make it look like we're getting something? It feels to me like you and all those other guys are caught in the middle of a totally convoluted set of circumstances organized by people (meaning diplomats and politicians, not servicemen) who don't know where they're going, let alone have any idea of how to get there.

It's not just you guys who are trapped, either. There are thousands upon thousands of us: family, friends, lovers, you name it! Can't they just get it over with? We need you back here. Don't worry, I won't try to turn this into another episode of "Couldn't you have foreseen this?" I don't want to end on that note.

It was a beautiful day today, so I had no trouble going in the ocean for the Feast of the Assumption. I'm going to guess you were not able to get to the beach. What else have you been up to? Those water trailers, do you have the same thing at your Las Vegas post? I can't imagine you would have running water.

Love,

Jane

Jane O'Brien

Spring Lake, New Jersey

August 16, 1970

Dear Michael,

I'm sorry about your attack. I'm glad you weren't hurt, and I don't mind getting a shorter letter than Sean did. I have no wish whatsoever to learn about fougasses or napalm or how enemy soldiers manage to get through barbed wire. I did need to know that a mortar shell missed you and that all the casualties were in the other battery, and you told me both of those things.

It was hot today, and I went to the beach. When I came home for lunch, your letter was here. I read it and then went to the Sea Girt beach off Chicago Boulevard where Sean goes. I found him and asked him to go back to your parents' house to see if he got a letter too. We found the letter, and he let me read it first. He then read it and went back to the beach. I came here to my parents' house, where I am now.

Everything's okay. You're right—I'm shaken by this and am not going back to the beach today, but I'd rather be shaken by knowing what happened than by not knowing. Please be careful.

Love,

Jane

Sean Ward

Sea Girt, New Jersey

August 16, 1970

Dear Mike,

That sapper attack really sounds like a night you won't forget. As you know, after graduating from ROTC, I took the Artillery Officer Basic Course at Fort Sill. While it was not part of the regular curriculum, the instructors there did discuss sapper attacks.

What they said was similar to what you were taught. We also were told that sappers never cut the barbed wire, since they're afraid of setting off trip flares. Maybe tying the wire with string before cutting it is a new technique. We were also told to stay under cover if satchel charges went off, because mortars were sure to follow. I guess you had a dramatic demonstration of that. I can't imagine what a string of fougasses going off simultaneously would be like. Just be careful.

Take care,

Sean

SP4 Michael Ward

Fire Support Base Las Vegas

Republic of Vietnam

August 16, 1970

Dear Jane,

I seem to be in trouble now, and it's ridiculous. Yesterday one of our infantry companies walked into an ambush and had to call in a fire mission to us. We plotted the location on the chart and worked up the figures, but we couldn't shoot because our numbers were different than the ones battalion came up with.

It took several minutes to figure out that battalion had a one-digit error in the grid coordinates they had written down. That delayed getting our shots out, and the infantry took some casualties during the interval.

After the mission ended, the battalion fire direction officer claimed that I had given them the wrong coordinates, which caused the delay, additional casualties, and a possible death. Lt. Fitzsimmons assured battalion he heard me call the location in correctly, but the S-3, a major, is siding with his people there. It doesn't look good.

Love,

Mike

Chapter 5
GRIDLOCK

Patrick Ward

Sea Girt, New Jersey

August 17, 1970

Dear Mike,

Well, Arnold Palmer has yet to win a PGA title. Yesterday's went to Dave Stockton. He was helped considerably by an eagle on the par 4 seventh hole when his 120-yard second shot dropped into the cup. Poor Arnold Palmer, his third time as runner-up! The days when one or two men dominated the field are gone.

I am going to be teaching Commercial Law II in the fall. As you may or may not know, that involves secured transactions under Article 9 of the Uniform Commercial Code. Most of the students are still taking their studies seriously, although some are becoming more and more radicalized. Unfortunately, a few of them seem to be wasting their time here, since protesting is all they seem to want to do.

I read your August 7 letter carefully and can't disagree with anything you say. Our war was very different. While our escort carriers did not gain ground, they did help to keep the sea lanes open and submarine-free enough to permit the freighters, tankers, and troop transports to get through, which ultimately led to ground gains. It may well be that all that our military forces can accomplish now is to give President Nixon something to hang his hat on to claim he had achieved his "peace with honor," even if that peace is incapable of lasting.

You are absolutely correct that what you're doing now is extremely, extremely critical. Your troop strength is dwindling, and our soldiers are at more and more risk each day. Every soldier who leaves renders those remaining less safe. The only way you can protect them and yourself is to do your job right. Make sure every calculation is correct and done quickly enough that you can return fire before the enemy can do much damage.

The enemy soldiers may not all be bad people and they may well be very brave, but the submarine crewmen we dealt with were probably brave and not evil either. They were, however, supporting a horrible institution that we could not destroy without going through them. We're not going to win this war, so your situation is not the same, but the enemy is the aggressor that invaded someone else's country, and all you're doing at this point is trying to get yourself and your friends out safely.

Affectionately,

Dad

SP4 Michael Ward

Fire Support Base Las Vegas

Republic of Vietnam

August 17, 1970

Dear Sean,

I don't know if Jane has spoken to you, but one of our missions got screwed up, probably because battalion made an error. Now they're trying to blame that error on me. They must have written the grid coordinates of a target down wrong, and they're claiming I radioed them the wrong figures. Now the S-3 is trying to claim the delay resulted in an infantryman getting killed and I'm to blame. At least I have witnesses here in our FDC, but the ones at battalion are higher ranking. It's a mess.

Take care,

Mike

Mrs. Patrick Ward

Sea Girt, New Jersey

August 20, 1970

Michael dear,

Your referring to powdered eggs brought back a lot of memories. That's all your father had on the ship. He wouldn't eat any type of scrambled eggs for nearly ten years after the end of the war.

It's been a beautiful week weather-wise. I've made it down to the beach a few times. Of course I go down there late and don't stay for very long. The night before last, we went to see the movie *Z*. It wasn't the easiest thing in the world to follow. It was very critical of Greek politics.

Lots of love,

Mom

SP4 Michael Ward

Fire Support Base Las Vegas

Republic of Vietnam

August 21, 1970

Dear Mom & Dad,

AFVN, the Armed Forces Vietnam Network, our one and only radio station, came on the air a little while ago. It goes off at midnight and comes back on at 6:00 a.m. The first thing you hear in the morning is "Goooooood morning, Vietnam!" The "Gooooooood" takes about twelve seconds. They play lots of different types of music during the day and night. Some of it is the rock you hear in New Jersey, but a lot of it is country-western. That music has a big following here. There's hardly any type of music, however, that doesn't have a half hour dedicated to it at some time of the week. Opera? Oh, yeah! Some military genius proposed that whites should listen to more soul music and blacks should listen to more country-western. This was supposed to lessen racial tensions. Edwin Smart wants nothing to do with it. He says forget about the country-western and just play Beethoven for all of us.

You should have about three more weeks of beach weather at the Jersey Shore. Fall is nice, though. I'd like to be able to put on a sweater and feel a cool breeze. Sweaters are one thing the army does not provide us with. I haven't heard any news about hurricanes in New Jersey, so maybe we'll get a break this year. Except for my time in the army, this was when I was always getting ready to go back to one school or another. That was the case for seventeen years, and it will be so again next year.

From what I hear, I'll have to dress differently then. Even the clothes we wore in college are archaic now. One good thing, the young people today seem to like wearing bits and pieces of military uniforms. Why, I don't know. At least I'll have plenty of those. Of course, nowadays you seem to have to mix an army field jacket with multicolored bell-bottoms. Eh!

Love,

Mike

Sean Ward

Sea Girt, New Jersey

August 22, 1970

Dear Mike,

It's late Saturday morning at the shore. I got down here last night. It looks like it's going to be a good weekend weather-wise. I went to Jimmy Byrne's last night and am waking up slowly. I'm heading to the beach in about an hour.

I see Agnew has called the troop withdrawal plan put forward by senators Hatfield and McGovern "a blueprint for the first defeat in the history of the United States." Then he went on: "One wonders if they really give a damn." He claimed that no more dangerous proposal had been made in the nineteen months that he had been in office—or in nineteen years, for that matter. Later in Washington, he went on to call the Cambodia invasion "the finest hour of the Nixon presidency." McGovern responded, "God save us from whatever may be his worst."

My own thoughts are mixed. There may be good reasons for not setting an inflexible withdrawal date, but raw insults are not going to lead to rational discourse on the subject. Also, if Agnew or anyone else in the administration wants a longer timetable, he needs to show what can be accomplished. His dialogue is notably short on that issue.

Take care of yourself,

Sean

Sean Ward

Sea Girt, New Jersey

August 23, 1970

Hey Mike,

I just got your 8/17/70 letter and brought it over to Jane. She had a more detailed one than I did this time. We both understand how consuming this problem must be. Don't worry. The truth usually finds a way of coming out. I have not mentioned it to Mom or Dad.

Take care,

Sean

Jane O'Brien

Spring Lake, New Jersey

August 23, 1970

Dear Michael,

I got your letter about the grid coordinates and

saw Sean's too. Yes, you've got to get this straightened
out. I'm glad you let me know. I have a great deal
of faith that things like this turn out in favor of the
person telling the truth, but no offense, there is a lesson to be learned here. Not everyone thinks like you,
Michael. You are where you are because you didn't
want your family connections to result in someone else
going in your place—but that other person, whoever
he might have turned out to be, wouldn't have hesi-
tated a second to do the same to you. You only have to
look at what this battalion officer is trying to do now
to learn how people behave in those situations. The
only thing that concerns him is covering his own ass.
He certainly isn't appreciating your moral commitment! I wish I could give him a piece of my mind, but
all I can do now is pray! Please let me know whatever happens.

Love,

Jane

SP4 Michael Ward

Fire Support Base Las Vegas

Republic of Vietnam

August 24, 1970

Dear Jane,

While our infantry companies can't hear battalion's radio transmissions because of the distance and

battalion can't hear theirs, they can both hear ours. We have high antennas like battalion's, but ours are much closer to the units in the field. It occurred to me that the forward observer would have been able to hear me when I relayed the coordinates he had just given me to battalion and probably would have noticed if they were different from what he had just sent. I couldn't ask him that over the radio, since battalion would hear me and probably accuse me of interfering with the investigation.

Now, guess what! Bravo Company, the one that called in the mission, arrived here yesterday to take over our perimeter security for a week. I found the forward observer, the reconnaissance sergeant, and the RTO, all of whom assured me that they always listen carefully to the calls when battery FDCs relay their data. They all verified they heard me call in the same grid coordinates they radioed to us, so the error had to have happened when battalion wrote them down. They also pointed out that the death occurred at the start of the ambush before they had even requested the fire mission, so it couldn't have been caused by the delay in getting fire support.

The forward observer had to come over to our FDC to use our radio to call battalion and tell them that. We haven't heard a word back. It's like they're pretending the whole thing never happened. Now that that worry is out of the way I have nothing to distract me from missing you!

I mentioned to a couple of the guys that I had written to you about the laundry girl who moonlights (or sunlights—she wouldn't be allowed on base after dark) providing amorous services for a price. They told me she nearly lost her mind the last time they changed the design of the military payment certificates, that she got stuck with over two thousand dollars of now-worthless MPCs. You really do have to feel sorry for her. Her career choice might not be the best, but she probably comes from a difficult background, and the loss of that much money here must be devastating. I'm still not sure what legitimate purpose these military payment certificates and the constant changes of design serve. Also, who gets the money she lost? I'm skeptical that it finds its way back into the military payroll.

Love,

Mike

SP4 Michael Ward

Fire Support Base Las Vegas

Republic of Vietnam

August 25, 1970

Dear Sean,

Yesterday morning we got an excited call in FDC from one of our own battery sergeants to contact Chu Lai right away. He and his gun crew could see rockets taking off from a nearby hilltop. They were all headed in that direction. We needed to alert Chu Lai to sound the alarm and to take cover.

As we were making the call, Lt. Fitzsimmons yelled out that we should try to destroy as many of the rockets as we could while they were still on the ground. Rather than working up firing data, he told the gun chief to just look down the bores of the gun tubes, aim them at the launch site like they were rifles, load, and fire. We managed to destroy most of the rockets that way before they took off. The infantry who responded there said that the rocket launchers were nothing more than crossed bamboo poles. The enemy would lay the front of a rocket on the crossed poles, light a fuse, and then get the hell out of the area.

AFVN is playing Neil Diamond's new song, *Cracklin' Rosie.* I seem to be the only one who thinks he's singing to a bottle of wine. Given the current popularity of the Portuguese "crackling" rosés, which don't have enough bubbles to be called "sparkling," I think I'm right.

As ever,

Mike

Barbara Connors
Cleveland, Ohio

August 26, 1970

Hi Michael,

You don't know who I am but, if you read on, you will. I better introduce myself. My name is Barbara Connors, and I work with Jill Fitzsimmons, David Fitzsimmons' sister. I believe David is a lieutenant in your unit. I asked Jill for the name and address of a soldier to write to, and she gave me yours, compliments of her brother.

I'm twenty-three years old and graduated from Penn State two years ago with a degree in fine arts. Since then I've been designing travel brochures for cruise lines. Ugh! Obviously, none of that work will ever be hung in the Museum of Contemporary Art, but I still paint a little on the side. Maybe someday something will come of that.

I hope you don't mind my writing to you. If you do, it's too late to do anything about it. It does make me feel like I'm doing something for you guys. It must seem like no one thinks about you, but we do. Don't get me wrong. I don't support the war, but we still have to care for the Americans that we sent there.

I really don't know much about the army or the war. It's very difficult to understand. There are newspaper articles and TV reports, but they tell you even less than watching a war movie, if that's possible. Then we have the war protesters. While I might agree with their position that we shouldn't have gone there in the first place, I don't like the way they say it. They seem to think they have the right to disrupt everyone else's lives just to make their point, even if the people whose lives their disrupting don't like the war either. They love to expound that they're at the forefront of some great new revolution, and yet they always lose the popular vote in every election.

I would like to hear what's happening where you are first hand. If you have the time and would like to write to me, I would enjoy that. If not, I understand. Above all, be careful!

Sincerely,

Barbara Connors

Mrs. Patrick Ward

Sea Girt, New Jersey

August 28, 1970

Michael dear,

Today is very hot, 90 degrees. These are the days that make me think we should have put air conditioning in this house. What's more important is that Tuesday is September 1st—one less month to go.

November 3 is Election Day. It will be the first Election Day since before Prohibition on which liquor will be allowed to be served in New Jersey. When Prohibition was repealed in 1933, our paternal legislature apparently decided that voting under the influence of alcohol could lead to unwise choices by the voters, so they made sure that couldn't happen. I'm not so sure that the choices they made cold sober were any better.

Perhaps if they served cocktails at the Paris Peace Conference, they would get some results. How long did they argue over whether the conference table would be square or round? Does anyone really believe that people who can't even agree on the shape of the table are capable of resolving anything?

Lots of love,

Mom

Jane O'Brien

Spring Lake, New Jersey

August 30, 1970

Dear Michael,

I just got your August 24 letter. For the first time in a while, I feel my prayers are really working. God bless those observer people. Now if you don't mind, I'm just going to drop that subject. I don't want to talk about it anymore.

I can't imagine being in a country and at the same time not being in that country, but that sounds like what you're doing. The Americans in Saigon may be a lot safer than you but apparently get to experience Vietnam more. No, I'm not talking about "meeting" the prostitutes, but they do get to walk around Vietnamese streets with Vietnamese people and eat

Vietnamese food in Vietnamese restaurants. I don't know what it was like for soldiers in World War II in Europe. Of course, while they were in England, they got to see the country, but how about after they crossed over into France? Then they may have lived more as you do, at least at first. What about the marines and soldiers in the Pacific during that war? They fought from island to island without ever knowing what they were like to visit in peacetime. Getting back to this war, though, there seem to be two types of Vietnam experiences, and it doesn't matter if you're officer or enlisted. There's the Vietnam that the Americans living in the cities see, and there's the Vietnam that you and your friends see.

When you get home, I'm going to take you to a Vietnamese restaurant in New York. It's ironic that I may have to do that to get you to taste Vietnamese food. I can't wait. I mean that. I really can't wait!

Love,

Jane

SP4 Michael Ward

Fire Support Base Las Vegas

Republic of Vietnam

August 30, 1970

Dear Jane,

We changed shifts today, so even though I'm now

on the noon-to-midnight shift, I had off from noon to 6:00 p.m. today. There was a supply truck heading back to Chu Lai at 1:00 p.m. Jim Kallin and I hitched a ride on it. That saved us from having to walk the two-mile dirt road to Route 1. When we finished what we were doing in Chu Lai, we waited at the main entrance to the base there for a truck heading north. The one that took us was going farther than we were and had to drop us off at the intersection of Route 1 and our dirt road. The pathway looks so insignificant I have trouble thinking of it as an intersection, but I don't know what else to call it. It was still light and we were armed with our M-16s, so the walk was uneventful.

While we were in Chu Lai, we got to the PX. I bought a pillow. We usually roll up something to put under our heads. We don't have regular bed covers either, so we use what are called poncho liners instead. They're like very thin, camouflage-colored quilts. The guys call them "baby blankets." They're comfortable, even in the heat.

We had to stop at our battalion FDC to pick up some grid coordinates that no one wanted to send over the radio even in code. Our big treat was that we got to stop at the USO and have some mint ice cream with hot fudge sauce. I can't remember the last time I had hot fudge sauce. Can you?

To respond to the comment in your letter, obviously someone got that slot in the reserves that I was offered. I don't know who that person was. I don't know if he was married with children. I don't know if he had a sick mother or father. I don't even know when he applied to get in the reserve. Maybe he had done his time on the waiting list. There's just no way I can evaluate this unidentified man's conduct.

Love,

Mike

Jane O'Brien

Spring Lake, New Jersey

August 30, 1970

Dear Michael,

I just got back from the beach. It was a nice day up until about one o'clock when it started pouring rain, and Angela and I had to rush into the Beach House at the Warren Hotel. We both had hot dogs and beer. Fortunately, we managed to get a table away from the door so that we didn't have to put up with greetings from every Tom, Dick, and Harry. We were still pestered more than we wanted. Is there really something about women with wet hair?

Last night Beth, Angela and I went to the Keynote at about ten o'clock. It was really crowded. They were playing traditional Irish stuff rather than anything current. This one guy wouldn't leave me alone, tried to hand me a drink I wouldn't take. Then he started bragging that he avoided the draft by convincing the army he was a drug addict. If one were to believe some of the newspaper articles, that would seem more like a necessary qualification. Anyway, I told him my boyfriend was in Vietnam. I went a little further than that even and pretended I was a real hawk. I told him he should listen to Vice President Agnew. That got rid of him. It's a good thing he didn't notice my Americans for Democratic Action card when I got out my driver's license.

I hope my little package arrives in time for your birthday. I made two different kinds of cookies in case you didn't like one of them. Then you can eat the ones you like and give the others away or eat them both or give them both away. Oh, what the hell, is this all I can do for you now?

Love,

Jane

SP4 Michael Ward

Fire Support Base Las Vegas

Republic of Vietnam

August 31, 1970

Dear Mom & Dad,

President Nixon is sending Vice President Agnew to Southeast Asia, including Vietnam. The announced purpose of his visit is to "reaffirm the conviction that the American presence in Southeast Asia is something we intend to maintain, and they depend on that." Nixon himself will be going to Europe.

I'm thinking of keeping my mustache. It does look pretty good. I guess the Jersey Shore is getting near the end of the season now. I will be looking forward to the next one.

Back some time ago, I read an article about Napoleon. When he graduated from the military academy in France, he surprised everyone by choosing to serve in the artillery rather than the cavalry. Most people thought that the cavalry was a better place for an ambitious officer. But Napoleon said he preferred the artillery because an artillery officer had to know everything happening on the battlefield and was therefore in a better position to learn battle tactics. I now know what he meant. Even as a spec 4, I know where every one of our units is at any given point in time. I know which ones are being attacked and from what direction, and I know ahead of time where helicopters are going to land with troops. I don't think even infantry company commanders have all that information.

It appears the barbers' union in Chicago is urging its members not to patronize stores that hire long-haired employees. Their stated rationale is they shouldn't give their business to people who aren't giving business to them. While their concern is legitimate, I don't think their plan will work.

Love,

Mike

SP4 Michael Ward

Fire Support Base Las Vegas

Republic of Vietnam

September 2, 1970

Dear Mom & Dad,

I've been reading *The Return of the King* by J.R.R.
Tolkien, part of *The Lord of the Rings* series. We now
have a Catholic chaplain, Father Malloy, a priest
from Pittsburgh who flies out here every Tuesday to
say Mass in our "club" building. It's decorated on the
inside with *Playboy* centerfolds. Father Malloy sees
nothing inappropriate in that. He feels it's just like the
paintings in the Sistine Chapel. He now comes and
gets me from the FDC bunker whenever he arrives so
I can do the scripture readings at Mass. Sometimes it
can be rough, if I've been on duty all night, but it does
restore some normalcy to my existence.

I was reading about the case of a marine officer
who stepped off a helicopter and was bitten by a king
cobra recently. There was a plan to use an Air Force
jet to fly in the director of the Miami Serpentarium,
who has been bitten by so many poisonous snakes that
he's developed an immunity. Transfusions from him
can transfer the immunity and have been used to save

other snake bite victims. Unfortunately, they couldn't get him here in time.

Love,

Mike

Jane O'Brien

Spring Lake, New Jersey

September 3, 1970

Dear Michael,

The summer is winding down, and I'll be back in school next week. It will feel good to be going back to work. Most people thought it was a good summer, but for me it wasn't. Last year we at least had two weeks together. There was nothing this year. For all the reading I've been doing, I could be a medieval monk (except they weren't reading on the beach in bikinis).

It must be very hot in VN right now. Do you spend much time in the sun, or are you altogether locked in your bunker? Write to tell me what you're doing. I was sorry to read what you said about that Vietnamese girl. Her life must have been awful before she lost the money, but at least she thought she was providing some security for herself. Now what does she have? What's the purpose of these military payment certificates, anyway? The soldiers have already paid the money out of those miserable little salaries you all get. They don't get that money back. Then the poor girl who demeans herself, probably to help her impoverished family, loses it as well. That money was appropriated to the army to pay military salaries. Who has it now?

By the end of the summer, I really wasn't hitting the night spots all that much. I had no desire to meet anyone or to drink too much. Next summer, let's visit a beach in another state. I love the New Jersey shore, but I feel that I'm just going to need something to shake me out of a stupor. How about Martha's Vineyard? I can't go through this again! I need you back here!

Love,

Jane

SP4 Michael Ward

Fire Support Base Las Vegas

Republic of Vietnam

September 5, 1970

Dear Barbara,

Thank you for your letter. It was nice of you to take the time to write. I've also thanked Lt. Fitzsimmons for giving you my name.

Don't feel bad about your present job. Your first position out of school very often isn't what you're looking for. The point is you have a job now and time to move around.

I never felt that our coming here was wrong in the moral sense. We were well intentioned, trying to stop one country from invading and taking over another. The problem is we're not accomplishing anything. Now even the generals are saying that "victory" was never possible. What are we doing then, and why did we come here? Whatever the problem is, the soldiers appreciate people who acknowledge we didn't cause it. It's very hard to explain what it feels like to be here, partly because no one arrives straight from civilian life. Everyone has to go through basic and advanced training, where in addition to being cold, wet, and sleep deprived, you're treated as being something subhuman, something that should have to apologize for existing. When you finally get to Vietnam and are treated like a valuable asset, someone who has an important job to perform, you're suddenly trans-formed from a useless, annoying creature to the cream of American youth. Of course, no matter how well you do your job, after a few months, you realize we're going absolutely nowhere. We give back every piece of ground we capture.

I'm now twenty-four. I graduated from college two years ago (Holy Cross). I even started law school before ending up in the army. I knew I was going to be drafted anyway, so I signed up under a delayed enlistment program that guaranteed I could finish the semester before being called to active duty. I plan to go back to law school after I get home. The army doesn't require returnees to finish out their service once they get back, probably because they have no particular use for anyone who doesn't have enough time left to be redeployed.

The whole enlistment thing did create a problem. While I did have to join something to avoid being drafted, I was offered a slot in the Army Reserve. If I had accepted that, I could have gone home after training and just attended meetings and summer camp. When I say my girlfriend was furious at me for not accepting the Army Reserve slot, I'm making a huge understatement. Our last dinner at home in a restaurant was a disaster. I'm no hero. It's just that I didn't think it was right that only people with poor connections had to bear the burden of this war. She and I are back writing to each other, but there have been some rough spots.

Thank you for listening to me. I hope I didn't bore you.

Sincerely,

Mike

Mrs. Patrick Ward

Sea Girt, New Jersey

September 6, 1970

Michael dear,

Let me start by wishing you a happy birthday! I have sent you some jelly candy. I know chocolate would be out of the question in your climate.

Labor Day is the absolute latest it can be this year, September 7. There was a big group of us sitting on the beach together today, including your cousin Bernadette as well as the whole Harrigan family, but by Tuesday it will all be over. Everyone will be back in school, me included. The one thing that makes me feel good about it is that when we start up another summer, you'll be here for it.

Last night was the annual Labor Day party at the golf club. We just had a small table with only your Uncle Peter and Aunt Patricia as guests. It was a beautiful night, so most of the food was cooked outdoors on the grill. We sat at a table inside. Of course everyone we spoke to was asking after you.

The latest news in Jersey City is that the buses are going to be requiring exact change now. This supposedly will cut down the number of robberies on bus drivers. It sounds like a nuisance, but if it works, it will be worth it.

Lots of love,

Mom

SP4 Michael Ward

Fire Support Base Las Vegas

Republic of Vietnam

September 9, 1970

Dear Mom & Dad,

I just read that yippie leader Jerry Rubin wrote a book called *Do It* in which he says young people of today should leave their homes, burn their schools, and then create a new society. Wouldn't that be a little difficult without any schools? Anyway, he's now setting up a tax-exempt foundation called the Social Education Foundation to receive the proceeds from the book. He feels it should be tax exempt because it "lessens the burden of government." The only trustee of the foundation is his wife. It seems to me that our situation in Vietnam and the protest against it have created a climate where any type of antiestablishment behavior, no matter how bizarre, is acceptable to some. Hopefully once the war is over, people will go back to analyzing things more rationally.

The weather is starting to cool off a little now. Before long, we'll be getting into the monsoon. A year ago I was at Fort Sill. That was a good training program there. They really taught us fire direction. It was hot there but also dry and not hard to get used to. It was a good break after all the mud we had to walk through, slip on, and fall down in at Fort Leonard Wood.

Love,

Mike

SP4 Michael Ward

Chu Lai

Republic of Vietnam

September 9, 1970

Dear Jane,

Unfortunately, we do spend a lot of time in our bunker. We work twelve-hour shifts and have to sleep sometime. That doesn't leave much time to be out in the sun. You can tell who's in FDC from who's on a gun crew just by how tan they are, at least the white guys.

I am in Chu Lai right now for an advanced fire direction course. There's a nice beach here, but we won't have time for it this time. We've gotten there for an hour or so a couple of times on our rare visits. It's on the South China Sea, and the water is calm because it is sheltered by the Philippine Islands. It's much more placid than the Atlantic Ocean at the Jersey Shore.

We do have a club building at Firebase Las Vegas, and we're allowed to have two beers a night if we're not on duty. I've very rarely had any. It doesn't sit well on my stomach. I hope that goes away when I leave. I may try to visit the club here in Chu Lai at the end of the week.

A lot of my work on the radio involves not just listening and talking but decoding grid coordinates.

Whenever an infantry company settles down in a new NDP (night defensive position), the forward observer sends us the location in code. We use our SOI (signal operating instructions) to interpret it. He also sends us a list of DTs (defensive targets) in the same manner. Defensive targets are locations from which the commander thinks his unit is likely to be attacked. We practice shooting at them in the evening so if there's an attack, all the fire adjustments will already have been calculated and we can hit the right spot with the first rounds.

Martha's Vineyard would be great, or the Jersey Shore, or anyplace other than Vietnam as long as you're there. For some reason, I miss you even more when I'm back in a classroom setting.

Love,

Mike

Jane O'Brien

Jersey City, New Jersey

September 10, 1970

Dear Michael,

I'm still happy with my job now that I'm back at work, but there seem to be a few dark clouds gathering. Not everyone is happy to have me as a replacement. There was an older teacher who went out on sick leave a few years ago who now wants to return, but the board is reluctant to let her. A group of the more senior staff here seems to think I got the position just because I'm young and attractive. I guess at least part of that is a compliment, but I'm not sure I want it. I put a lot of effort into being a good teacher, not to mention my training and education. I take it seriously, and they should take me seriously. Perhaps I'm more worried that they may be right. I don't like the way the principal looks at me like I'm on a dessert tray. That's bad enough, but there's something else I want to ask you about.

Last week a group of Vietnam veterans who are opposed to the war demonstrated in Bernardsville. They had people planted in the audience, mostly women, whom they proceeded to grab, terrorize, and shout obscenities at. They said this is what they did in Vietnam. Michael, is there anything else you're not telling me? I agree that this doesn't sound like you, but you're there. What's happening? I may not be interested in fougasses or whatever, but I was shocked to learn of this.

I'm not going to respond directly to your comments about the other man who got the reserve spot you were offered other than to say you're a dreamer, Michael. For someone so smart you're very naïve.

Love,

Jane

Mrs. Patrick Ward

Jersey City, New Jersey

September 12, 1970

Michael dear,

    I'm at school. The boy who picks up the school's mail at the post office just brought in a letter from you addressed to the house. This is the second time this has happened. Someone at the post office must know I work here. Never worry that your letters might be boring. One word on a sheet of paper coming from you would make the day bright for Dad and me. Incidentally, I mailed five books to you Friday. I guess the one good thing about your situation is that you do get to read a lot. There's an adage that war is endless boredom followed by moments of terror.

    Eddie Borden was home from Korea for his father's funeral. He expected to go back but has been reassigned to Fort Monmouth as a type of hardship case. Your father said he didn't like the gleam in my eye when he told me that. He's afraid I'm going to do him in to get you home.

    By the time you get this, four months of your stay will be over. God speed the rest.

Lots of love,

Mom

Barbara Connors

Cleveland, Ohio

September 13, 1970

Dear Mike,

You didn't bore me at all, but I have some advice to give you. Do you remember the Richard Lovelace poem that concludes:

"I could not love thee, dear, so much,

Loved I not honour more."

Well, if you do remember it, then forget it. No woman wants to hear that her guy thinks it's okay for him to leave her just so some other guy doesn't have to do the same thing to some other woman. You have some serious fences to mend still.

Sincerely,

Barbara

Chapter 6
SCHOOL BELL BLUES

SP4 Michael Ward

Fire Support Base Las Vegas

Republic of Vietnam

September 13, 1970

Dear Sean,

I had my advanced fire direction training in Chu Lai last week. The course was good and made me feel a lot more confident. There were some not good parts about being in Chu Lai, though. I made one visit to the EM Club. Never again. A frat party would seem tame by comparison. The worst thing by far in Chu Lai, however, was the drugs and the people on them. For all the talk, I'd never seen drugs in Vietnam before this, but they're definitely there in Chu Lai. Of course, if you listen to the DOD's entertainment office, all of the soldiers here are turned on to pot smoking and rock music. That's why they're considering dropping

The Bob Hope Show. What they probably mean is that the GIs they see are like that. Somehow, I don't expect either *The Bob Hope Show* or the people who book it to make it out to where we are.

I'm upset about the publication of Lindbergh's wartime journal. The man was a national hero at one time. Now it appears he had said we were on the wrong side in World War II. He even accepted a medal from the Nazis and blamed the war on President Roosevelt, Britain, and Jewish propagandists. Before reading about it, I thought at least World War II veterans didn't have to put up with crap like that.

As ever,

Mike

SP4 Michael Ward

Fire Support Base Las Vegas

Republic of Vietnam

September 16, 1970

Dear Jane,

Concerning the show you mentioned by the veterans in Bernardsville: I'm not in the infantry, and I don't go from village to village in remote areas. I have walked from Fire Base Las Vegas around the neighboring villages along Route 1 and have encountered numerous Vietnamese. I've always been armed with an M-16 rifle, as are my buddies, and no one has demonstrated any fear of us. All our lieutenants have worked as forward observers with the infantry, and none of them agree with the scenarios demonstrated in Bernardsville. That being said, the Mekong Delta is as far from us here as South Carolina is from New Jersey. We know about as much about what's happening there as you do about what's happening in Charleston now. I can't say what other people did or didn't experience during their tours of duty. I'm not saying the types of things described didn't happen, only that they're not as universally prevalent as suggested. What you relate does not seem typical, at least to me, and I think you should have realized that!

Within the past week, Vice President Agnew has castigated "caterwauling critics" and "nattering nabobs of negativism." His overfondness for alliteration is indicative of some misplaced fantasy that the mere process of starting every word with the same letter will somehow transform verbal rubbish into fine rhetoric. I don't know which is worse, the far left or the far right. At least the right claims they like us soldiers, but then they think that "once you've seen one slum, you've seen them all" and that the country's real problem is pornography.

Today is Monday, big pill day. There are small malaria pills we take every day and then a big one we take once a week. We have to stand in formation to receive and take the latter since some men have tried to skip it to catch malaria and spend some time in the hospital.

Love,

Mike

SP4 Michael Ward

Fire Support Base Las Vegas

Republic of Vietnam

September 16, 1970

Dear Mom & Dad,

Did you know that the Americal Division is the only American army division never to have served in the United States? It was created in New Caledonia in World War II. If it is pulled out of a foreign war zone like Vietnam to go back to the States, it ceases to be a division and reverts to being various unattached brigades. Because it can serve only in southern regions, its insignia is the Southern Cross, the constellation. Its motto is "Under the Southern Cross." The shoulder patch is in the shape of a shield. On dress uniforms, the background is blue and the stars are white. On the combat uniforms we wear here, the background is olive drab and the stars are black. No other American army division has suffered the losses that ours has in this war.

What happened in My Lai was a tragedy I still cannot comprehend, and it will be with us forever, but I still can't put aside the devotion and suffering of so many of the soldiers who have served "under the

Southern Cross." I will have that with me forever, too. I don't mean to be preaching, but sometimes I feel most of what really happens here gets lost in what others consider the bigger story.

Love,

Mike

Jane O'Brien

Jersey City, New Jersey

September 16, 1970

Dear Michael,

The principal is getting to be a little more of a concern. Today at lunchtime he told me he wanted to meet with me after work to review my progress. Okay so far! So I told him I'd come to his office after dismissal. No, he wanted me to meet him in the cocktail lounge at Pedro's so he could have a drink to unwind after school. So how to tell him I was not going to go without just saying he was an old lech? I told him it was too early in the day for me to have a drink, but I could join him for coffee at the diner. He didn't want to do that, so I just came home afterward. I hope that's the end of it.

I'm sorry if I'm not too chatty today. I just wanted to tell you about this. I see that your troop strength is now down to 396,300. Do you really believe it would have made any difference if it were 396,299?

Love,

Jane

Mrs. Patrick Ward

Jersey City, New Jersey

September 18, 1970

Michael dear,

I just got home from school. After your father gets back, we are going to head down the shore and have dinner at the golf club. Your father is going to play golf tomorrow. I would just like to sit in the backyard. It should be a nice day. I'm a little worried about Bernadette. She's not taking her mother's death well. Maybe she shouldn't, but she needs to get her own life back on track. It hasn't been good for the last year, understandably. She needs a real outside job.

I know some news can be strange, but a seventeen-year-old girl in Florida just gave birth to a child. The father and her husband, whose name is Walter Lee Martin Jr., is fifteen years old and a Vietnam veteran who has been wounded twice. He lied about his age and was only twelve when he enlisted. He doesn't sound anything like the young men who have fled to Canada.

Lots of love,

Mom

SP4 Michael Ward

LZ Liberty Bell

Republic of Vietnam

September 19, 1970

Dear Jane,

We're on another jump now. We had to leave so quickly I didn't get a chance to write anyone. This base has barbed wire but not much else. It's near the coast south of Chu Lai, not far from My Lai. The area is called Batangan Peninsula. We haven't had any attacks on our position. I don't have much time.

Love,

Mike

SP4 Michael Ward

LZ Liberty Bell

Republic of Vietnam

September 20, 1970

Dear Sean,

We've been out on another jump for the past three days and are going back to Firebase Las Vegas tomorrow. Where we are now is near the coastline south of Chu Lai. We came with a full infantry battalion as a backup to the troops that were already here. The purpose of the move was to trap a Viet Cong unit believed to be operating in the area. I'm not sure whether we found it or not.

This morning, a forward observer called in a fire mission on a large number of "Mike Alpha Mikes" (military-aged males) who appeared to be fleeing the area by water in open boats. I took the call, gave the coordinates to our team to plot and compute, and called it in to our battalion FDC. I had to relay the call because the prick-25s carried by the forward observers aren't powerful enough to reach Chu Lai. Battalion told me to ask the forward observer if he could see any weapons in the boats. I did, and he said it was impossible to see that well in the distance. As a result, battalion denied us clearance to shoot. But I have to suspect what the forward observer saw was actually the unit we were looking for. By the time I finished my calls, I was surrounded by officers who couldn't believe what was happening. They felt this was the whole reason we were here. For all the talk about My Lai, which is not far from here, I doubt anyone ever reports how extraordinarily careful we are in reality.

Except for the fact that this LZ does have barbed wire, it's less hospitable even than LZ Hurrah. We have a small structure to use as an FDC with radio antennas, but there was nowhere for us to sleep, so we had to dig foxholes, which we covered with dirt-filled wooden ammunition boxes as protection from mortars. You wouldn't believe the number of crawling insects that find their way into those holes. The scari-est-looking are the tropical centipedes. They're about eight inches long and thick as a man's index finger. Their bodies are dark blood red with white curled legs. The cockroaches we used to see in college dorms seem like household pets by comparison. Sweet dreams!

We're eating C rations, but they had no heating tabs to give us, so we're using C-4 to warm them. Simply lighting it with a match won't cause it to blow up; it just burns. We've been warned not to step on it to put it out. That would cause it to explode, and it would blow your foot off.

As ever,

Mike

Jane O'Brien

Jersey City, New Jersey

September 21, 1970

Dear Michael,

Our principal is no longer a problem. Imagine that! At least he speaks with me in a matter-of-fact fashion now, without leering, and hasn't suggested any further questionable "professional" meetings. It seems I had a little backup. Jeremy made some remarks to carefully chosen people saying he'd seen me com-ing from an attorney's office in the Trust Company Building. That attorney has had his name in the paper recently for winning a big sexual harassment suit. You probably don't know what that is, but Jeremy is going to law school at night and said they are starting to become the thing. Apparently, even the suggestion of the possibility of such a suit was enough to scare the pants off you know who (or vice versa, as the pants may be). The truth of the matter is that I didn't visit an attorney at all. I was going to the dentist in that building when Jeremy saw me, so he decided to improvise a little for my benefit.

For as much as my graduate courses dealt with teaching in the classroom, it's impossible to be completely removed from the children's lives outside of school. Kids who come from a background of violence or substance abuse in the home can't just sit down and do their homework the way we did. I wanted to talk to one of the mothers about her child's failure to complete assignments. After she missed our first two appointments, I became more assertive. She finally showed up with a poorly disguised black eye covered with a lot of makeup. Homework was not her principal worry. I tried to ask her what happened, but she was evasive. I know we're supposed to report suspected child abuse to the Bureau of Children's Services, but I don't think there's any equivalent for adults. In any event, the very next day a man came up to me in the parking lot after school and told me to stop bothering his wife. I don't know if this was the husband of the woman with the black eye, but I was scared. Fortunately, Jim Hughes popped right over and asked what was going on, and the man hustled off without one further word. I don't think abusers are brave. Thank God for my fellow teachers.

Love,

Jane

SP4 Michael Ward

Fire Support Base Las Vegas

Republic of Vietnam

September 22, 1970

Dear Jane,

Andy Winberry just got back from his R&R. Supposedly he was going to Hawaii to meet his girlfriend, but she was waiting for him at his home in Oregon. Once he got to Honolulu, he boarded another plane for the mainland and continued on. He could have gotten in a lot of trouble if he'd been caught. For someone on R&R, leaving Hawaii to go to the mainland is considered going AWOL. But he made it, and he's telling everyone about it now. The officers here don't care, as long as he came back. No one ever gets angry at him, anyway. He's one of those guys who seems to have a perpetual grin on his face. What strikes me as funny is why they wouldn't have chosen to meet in Hawaii. I know Oregon is supposed to be a beautiful state, but Hawaii just seems so much more romantic. What do you think?

On another front, I see that Williams College has just begun its first semester with female students. When we started college a mere six years ago, I don't think anyone could have foreseen all the changes that would take place.

I guess the summer is really over in New Jersey. The bars with the six-month licenses have until October 15, but I can't imagine they'll be too busy. It makes me feel good to think that I will be there when they reopen. Let's go to Jimmy Byrne's opening night and stay until closing.

Love,

Mike

SP4 Michael Ward

Fire Support Base Las Vegas

Republic of Vietnam

September 24, 1970

Dear Mom & Dad,

Bill Davis went home to Georgia yesterday, not that Georgia was where he grew up. His father was a career NCO in the army, so he lived everyplace from Oklahoma to Germany as a kid. When Bill graduated from high school, he came right into the army. He's leaving now to go to college, where he plans to take ROTC. I guess he'll be back in uniform before too long, which should be a good thing. His military

knowledge was incredible. He could name every air-
craft in the sky, every vehicle on the ground, and every
weapon they carried as well as how they operated.
None of the lieutenants could match him. With all
that, you'd think he would be a gung-ho type, but he
wasn't. He was just very exact, cautious, and dedicated.
A good man to learn from!

With his leaving, however, I am now the chief
computer on our shift, so I won't be doing too much
more radio work. I'm enjoying the change. It's unusual
for the chief computer to be a SP4. Bill was a sergeant.
Everyone is getting ready for the monsoon and the
colder weather now.

Love,

Mike

Mrs. Patrick Ward

Jersey City, New Jersey

September 24, 1970

Michael dear,

It has been very hot here lately. There have even
been some brownouts. We are going to be heading
down the shore tomorrow evening. Who knows? We
might even get to the beach over the weekend.

A reporter for *Newsweek* has filed suit against
the army in federal court. He claims he was called
to active duty in the reserve because he wrote an

unfavorable article about Judge Harrold Carswell and his nomination to the United States Supreme Court. The army says the real reason he was called up was that he had missed too many reserve unit meetings. You do have to give him credit for coming up with this angle.

Lots of love,

Mom

Jane O'Brien

Jersey City, New Jersey

September 26, 1970

Dear Michael,

I was reading the paper the other day and saw what you meant about "big pill day." The United States reported 3,806 new cases of malaria in 1969. All but 127 of them were military personnel. The same article cited the failure of many of the men to take the preventive medication as a cause but said their failure was a based on a feeling of invincibility. I think your reason sounds more likely.

I can't stop thinking about when we went fishing in South Carolina. I didn't mind fishing and I liked reeling in the fish, but I couldn't put the bait on the hook. I had to have you do that. I guess what made me think of it was what you told Sean about your centipedes. I'm not upset that you didn't mention that to me this time because I know why you didn't, but at the same time, for future reference, I do want to know about those things even if I won't put a worm on a hook. I do want to know what your life is like there.

Love,

Jane

SP4 Michael Ward

Fire Support Base Las Vegas

Republic of Vietnam

September 30, 1970

Dear Sean,

I had a rough wake-up very early this morning. I was sound asleep until I felt someone shaking me violently. Then I realized it was Lt. Baker, the fire direction officer on the other shift. He kept asking me if I was all right. I couldn't understand why until I saw there was dirt from the roof all over the floor, and all our "lockers" (made from wooden ammunition boxes) had been knocked off the walls. We had taken a direct hit from a mortar, and I slept right through it. The sound of the mortar hitting our roof was probably much softer than the racket we're used to hearing when the full battery fires.

It appears the NVA had been planning a sapper attack that didn't get very far. Some of them snuck got through the wire, but then the dogs heard them and started barking. There was an exchange of gunfire before any explosives could be set off. The NVA mortar crew started to fire, because they knew their cover was blown. Our battery was the one to be targeted this time. Even though nothing got blown up, the guy with the AK-47 did some damage. Several guys were wounded. (One didn't make it!)

We learned something else the hard way, too. The firing battery attempted to shoot back at the mortars with "beehive" rounds. Those are sort of like shotgun shells for cannons. They contain multiple flechettes that look like darts. They're intended for use close up, such as when an artillery battery is the target of a ground attack. They're like the grapeshot they used to have in old muzzle-loading cannons. Anyway, we weren't prepared for what it did to our barbed wire. As a matter of fact, after the guns fired, there was no barbed wire left on that side of the firebase. The flechettes completely destroyed all of it.

It also made me think back to the martini incident when Capt. Berlen had us add two more layers of sandbags to the roof of our bunker. I hate to think what would have happened if he hadn't had us do that.

As ever,

Mike

SP4 Michael Ward

Fire Support Base Las Vegas

Republic of Vietnam

September 30, 1970

Dear Jane,

Andy Winberry died this morning. It's a good thing he got to see his girlfriend in Oregon. The NVA staged an "unsuccessful" sapper attack here. They didn't get to set off any explosive satchel charges, but there was automatic weapons fire. Andy woke up when a mortar hit our FDC. He heard AK-47 fire nearby (very distinctive, a much higher-pitched crackle than an M-16) and rushed up to the door to keep the sapper from getting inside. He wasn't wearing his helmet or his flak jacket. There wasn't time. He was hit with a bullet before one of the guys on a gun crew shot the sapper. I wasn't injured. I'll miss him and his good nature.

Our mail arrived anyway. I don't feel like talking about it after what happened here, but I'm glad your principal backed off, and I'm even grateful to your friend for the imaginative way he helped. I appreciate what your other friend did as well. Your letter included a few backhanded comments, though. You're well aware that I'm going to law school too. I do know what a sexual harassment lawsuit is, and had I been there, I would have done something. I know you're unhappy about what I'm doing, and you know what? Right now it's kind of miserable for me too.

Love,

Mike

Chapter 7
A BOMB

Mrs. Patrick Ward

Jersey City, New Jersey

September 30, 1970

Michael dear,

I'm sorry to have to tell you that your Godmother Marjorie died last evening at the Jersey City Medical Center. The funeral will be later this week. The family assures me that your candle will stay where it is until you come home.

We just came through a very bad heat wave, very unusual for this time of year. There were some power outages, but we're back to normal now. I will let you know how things go with the funeral.

Lots of love,

Mom

Patrick Ward

Jersey City, New Jersey

October 2, 1970

Dear Mike,

I see that in preparation for Presidents Nixon's visit to Ireland, it's been revealed that he's part Irish. That's not something I would have anticipated. He's even going to visit the grave of his great, great, great, great, great-grandfather Milhous in the old Quaker graveyard at Timahoe, County Kildare. Will he want to join the Friendly Sons of St. Patrick next?

There are news reports of a big combat base being turned over by the marines to the South Vietnamese Army. It's at Anhoa, twenty miles southwest of Danang. That should put it not too far from you. Apparently, the First Marine Division is being withdrawn to Camp Pendleton, California, one regiment at a time. It should all be gone by May 1971 except for one brigade left to guard Danang. There seem to be fewer and fewer American servicemen staying behind.

The new semester is well underway at the law school. Every year, the students seem more and more ragged. It wasn't that long ago that law students had to dress as if they were working in a law office. That's certainly not the case now. For the most part, their academic interest is still strong, and the vast majority of the students are serious about their studies. But if anyone were to read the posters all over the school, they might get a completely different impression, that all the students were doing was protesting one thing or another. It's not just about antiwar activities; there are civil rights, women's rights, abortion rights, you name it. Students have always had these concerns, but now it's more confrontational.

Your mother and I will be going down to the shore Saturday night after the funeral. It's not supposed to be terribly warm, but it won't be cold either and it should be clear, good weather for golf. We'll also probably get to the club for dinner. We ran into the Robinsons Tuesday night at The Alps. Their son just got back from Vietnam two months ago. He was in the artillery too, but down south in the Mekong Delta. Stay cautious.

Affectionately,

Dad

SP4 Michael Ward

Fire Support Base Las Vegas

Republic of Vietnam

October 3, 1970

Dear Jane,

I've been in Vietnam almost five months now. In another month, people will start looking at me like I'm an old sage. I'm even beginning to feel like one.

My R&R will be coming up near the end of November. It may well include Thanksgiving weekend. I want to spend it with you in Hawaii. If you could persuade the board of education to let you take three personal days, you could meet me in Honolulu. Even if they say no, you can come for a long weekend. I know it's far, but it's all I can think about, especially after what happened to Andy. I'm going to put in for Hawaii now. Please get back to me on this.

The monsoon is really in full force now. The cold weather is welcome, but the rain is a nuisance. It is also delaying our mail considerably, so please keep this in mind in responding. Lt. Fitzsimmons was chosen as Americal Division Lieutenant of the Week, so he's in Chu Lai today having lunch with the general.

Love,

Mike

Mrs. Patrick Ward

Jersey City, New Jersey

October 3, 1970

Michael dear,

I saw a picture in the paper of some GIs in the rain. Oh, how it made me think of you and your conditions. I guess it's that time of year in Vietnam. Of course, we don't have a monsoon in New Jersey, but you'll be happy to know that we converted our heat from oil to gas. It seems to be working very well. There's even heat in the radiator in your room. That's something! Now while you're standing in the rain, you can think about how warm and comfortable you'll be next winter.

I was supposed to go to Marjorie's funeral today, but I'm here waiting for the plumber instead. The toilet in the powder room isn't working, and we can't leave it that way. Tomorrow is supposed to be a fair weather, so we're going back to the shore tonight (provided the plumber comes).

It's been a long while since we had a letter from you. I'm sure you're writing. The monsoon must be holding up the mail. Betty McGill is going to England on the Queen Elizabeth 2. As much as I would like to take a cruise too, I'm not doing anything until you're home.

I just read in the paper that President Nixon has a new plan for rapid troop withdrawals. I hope it works. Any plan that gets all of you home soon is a good one.

Lots of love,

Mom

SP4 Michael Ward

Fire Support Base Las Vegas

Republic of Vietnam

October 4, 1970

Dear Mom & Dad,

Well, the monsoon has certainly slowed down our mail. No planes have been taking off or landing. A big batch of mail came in today, the first in about five days. Strangely, one of the letters I received was postmarked August 17. The cool weather here is welcome now, although we could do without the rain. It's causing some flooding here in our bunker. We can still operate the FDC but may have to sleep somewhere else.

Thank you for the new restaurant brochure. It's funny how enjoyable it is to look at things like that. A rack of lamb seems pretty good about now.

The US seems to be having troubles all over the place. I read that leftist gangs in Rome are setting fire to cars with American license plates to protest President Nixon's visit. Somehow I doubt that even an old "Humphrey for President" bumper sticker would have helped much.

I also see that the United States has denied a visa to former Cuban dictator Batista to attend his brother's funeral in Florida. What seems to be generating more sparks, however, is whether South Vietnamese Vice President Nguyen Cao Ky should attend the March for Victory rally in Washington. Congressman Dorn of South Carolina, a Democrat, wanted him to come, while (of all people) Vice President Agnew did not. Dorn even compared it to having Kosygin at Glassboro State College in New Jersey. Since the march was scheduled for yesterday, I guess that has all been resolved by now.

I'm back on the midnight-to-noon shift, so breakfast will be in about four hours. We haven't had any calls for fire support from any of our units in the field. It's quiet. Lt. Col. Jordan, our new battalion commander, is spending the night here. We're on our best military behavior, even carrying rifles in the shower.

Love,

Mike

Patrick Ward

Jersey City, New Jersey

October 8, 1970

Dear Mike,

Your mother and I were glued to the television last night for President Nixon's address about Vietnam. He called for an immediate cease-fire, not just for Vietnam but all of Indochina, including Cambodia and Laos. He then went on to propose international supervision of the cease-fire as a preliminary to ending the entire war. He asserted that there has been a marked drop in US casualties as our troop strength in Indochina has been reduced. It reached its peak in February 1968 at 542,500 and is now down to 384,000.

I guess the question on everyone's mind is why North Vietnam would ever agree to this. If we weren't able to keep things under control with all our troops there, how can we possibly do so now? They want to take over the south, and they are not going to agree to anything that keeps them from doing just that. Hopefully, the casualty rate will continue to get lower.

The president did point out that there has never been any real peace in the world since World War II. There has always been fighting somewhere. He then opined that the cease-fire in the Middle East could spread to Indochina and there would be world peace for the first time in a generation. I'm not even sure how long the Middle East peace will last.

Affectionately,

Dad

Jane O'Brien

Jersey City, New Jersey

October 8, 1970

Dear Michael,

I'm sorry about Andy. I had to put your letter down to catch my breath. You asked earlier what I thought about him and his girlfriend meeting in Oregon instead of Hawaii, which is more romantic. I think it was because, if they were in Hawaii, they wouldn't have been able to put out of their minds that in a few days he was going back to Vietnam, and she was going back to the mainland. At least in Oregon they could pretend that it was not so. For her sake I think it's better that her last memories of him will be from home.

I did not mean to belittle your legal training, but how is it helping? You could be Perry Mason come to life, and it wouldn't do any good if you weren't here. I do so wish you were.

Love,

Jane

SP4 Michael Ward

Fire Support Base Las Vegas

Republic of Vietnam

October 9, 1970

Dear Mom & Dad,

Dad mentioned that you ran into the Robinsons at dinner at The Alps the other night and they said Terry had been in the artillery in the Mekong Delta. While that's far from us, we strangely have had some communication with people there. We often have to change the radio frequencies we operate on so the North Vietnamese won't know which unit is on which frequency. Since there are a limited number of such frequencies (or "pushes," as we call them), and since the Mekong Delta is so far from us and normally out of radio range, we sometimes use the same push that they do down there. Every so often, usually on a cloudy day, the radio waves will bounce in a strange fashion and we find ourselves talking to an artillery unit down in IV Corps in the Delta for a limited time. I have no way of knowing if he was one of those people. We certainly don't give names.

Several days ago, we were warned there was going to be a B-52 strike in our area. The bombs those planes carry are enormous. When the time came, however, we didn't hear any explosions. All we noticed was an increase in air pressure, like when you're landing on an airplane. Anyhow, the guys on the other FDC shift, who had been asleep, came running out yelling, wanting to know what was going on. We hadn't thought to wake them up to tell them what was going to happen.

We are going to show *The Molly Maguires* tonight with Sean Connery and Catherine Ross.

Love,

Mike

Mrs. Patrick Ward

Sea Girt, New Jersey

October 11, 1970

Michael dear,

Your letter of October 4 came yesterday and was delightedly received. I felt so bad when the flood took over your villa. We are still coming down here on the weekends and will continue to do so for a short while. Yesterday was so warm there were people on the beach—unusual for October. Today is gloomy. Your father is at 10:15 Mass; I went at five o'clock yesterday. I do that most of the time now so I can work on the *Times* Sunday morning crossword. We had dinner at Pals Aweigh last night and ran into Betty McGill. She couldn't believe you had been in Vietnam five months already. I can. She said she wishes you could be home by Christmas. I told her whatever day you do come home will be Christmas.

Tomorrow is Columbus Day, so it's a long weekend. I'm going to be doing your father's wash-and-wear suit. (Drat the thing!) I should go shopping with him to make sure he doesn't buy another.

Lots of love,

Mom

SP4 Michael Ward

Fire Support Base Las Vegas

Republic of Vietnam

October 12, 1970

Dear Sean,

The mess hall blew up last night. Everyone thought it was an incoming mortar round, but it wasn't. The MPs are here. It was a bomb. It was planted here, but no one knows who did it or why. Could it have been one of the few Vietnamese allowed on the base? Could it have been one of our own soldiers? It was after dinner and no one in the building at the time, but who knows when the bomb was planted? Everyone is real nervous. If it happened once, it can happen again unless they catch the person who did it.

The North Vietnamese have rejected President Nixon's cease-fire proposal. They are saying it would legalize American aggression in Indochina. Am I missing something? We are agreeable to leaving if North Vietnam leaves too. North Vietnam is not willing to go, however, even if we do. How does that make us the aggressor? Happy Columbus Day!

As ever,

Mike

SP4 Michael Ward

Fire Support Base Las Vegas

Republic of Vietnam

October 12, 1970

Dear Jane,

Happy Columbus Day! We have a situation here. A bomb went off in our mess hall last night. No one was hurt. The MPs say it was a homemade bomb like the Viet Cong use. It has everyone on edge. No GI would have something like that, but it's hard to imagine that a Vietnamese could have planted it without being noticed. So then who did? I figured you'd want to know about this.

We're getting plenty of rain these days, and it has cooled off somewhat. We can even wear shirts (or bush jackets, as they call them) in the bunker. Back home, I always like this time of year. The summer heat has passed, and the winter cold hasn't arrived yet.

Love,

Mike

Jane O'Brien

Jersey City, New Jersey

October 13, 1970

Dear Michael,

Your letter did take longer to arrive. Bad monsoon! I will put in for three personal days, but I'm not optimistic. After all, I'm new here.

Speaking of which, it seems the newest person always has the pleasure of arranging the teachers' holiday dinner. I have lately been spending my free time trying to find an appropriate location. Of course, that involves looking at menus and prices. I've been told by the last few lucky ones that it's impossible to do right. If you pick the better items, some people will complain about the price. If you go for the lower prices, others will complain about the quality of the food. Oh, and do you know how to go about hiring an accordion player?

I was reading a newspaper article the other day about racial problems with the US Army in Germany. Apparently, it is really getting out of hand. Some of the difficulty is with the Germans who don't want to rent to black GIs or serve them in bars and restaurants, but some of it is with white soldiers too. There have even been cross burnings. The black soldiers are giving black power salutes with raised fists rather than normal military ones. Does anything like that happen in Vietnam? I can't imagine you could fight a war with that type of internal hostility.

Every time I see your mother, she asks if I've heard from you and the date of your last letter. She never asks what you said. She probably feels that would be too intrusive. She just wants to know you're still well enough to write a letter.

Love,

Jane

Mrs. Patrick Ward

Jersey City, New Jersey

October 15, 1970

Michael dear,

Well, Columbus Day is over, and we're back in Jersey City. Soon Halloween will be here and gone, and we'll be that much closer to your coming home. It seems I spent a good part of the holiday rounding up cookie tins for the St. Mark's card party. One of my Mass friends asked me if I had any. She was delighted when she saw how many I had tucked away that were the perfect size. Our attic holds something for everyone. Now she wants me to sit at her table.

Your letter arrived. I can hardly wait for Dad to arrive to see it. We can spend an evening reading and discussing one letter. Everyone wants to know why your APO number keeps changing even though you're still at the same place. The army post office seems to perform like the rest of the army.

One of our local congressional elections is picking up a lot of steam. Congressman Daniels is running for reelection against an administrator from Essex County College named Carlo De Gennero. Mr. De Gennero says that he supports President Nixon's policy of "Vietnamization." How is it that one goes about "Vietnamizing" Vietnam? If that means getting you and the other Americans out of there, I'm all for it.

Lots of love,

Mom

SP4 Michael Ward

Fire Support Base Las Vegas

Republic of Vietnam

October 15, 1970

Dear Mom & Dad,

Well first we have Gen. Westmoreland saying no American military leaders ever believed that a classical military victory was possible for us in Vietnam. Now we have Deputy Secretary of Defense David Packard saying that the North Vietnamese will have to accept Nixon's cease-fire proposal because they're losing ground militarily while the US is making excellent progress. How do we reconcile these two apparently contradictory statements? If asked to do so, I suppose the administration would say the US is making excellent progress but only in the nonclassical sense! Here at Firebase Las Vegas, we'll have to keep in mind that we are now engaged in a nonclassical war! Does that mean that we're allowed to shoot only nonclassical artillery? I guess that's why President Nixon announced on Monday that he will have forty thousand more troops home by Christmas. That's only ten weeks away. It's going to start getting lonely here.

I see the 1970 Nobel Prize for Literature is going to Aleksandr Solzhenitsyn for his novel *One Day in the Life of Ivan Denisovich.* Solzhenitsyn was an artillery-man himself, a battery commander who was captured by the Germans in World War II. A letter he wrote as a POW led to his receiving an eleven-year sentence in the Soviet Union after the war ended. His prison experience served as the basis for the novel in question. It's unlikely the Soviets will let him go to Sweden to accept the award. They didn't let Boris Pasternak go to accept the award for *Dr. Zhivago.*

We registered a new gun today. The tubes on our guns wear out and have to be replaced from time to time. Whenever one of them is changed, we have to register it, meaning we have to shoot some rounds to see if the projectiles travel the distance they're supposed to, according to the firing tables. There are sometimes slight variations we record and adjust for.

They're starting to serve lunch, so I have to get over there.

Love,

Mike

SP4 Michael Ward

Fire Support Base Las Vegas

Republic of Vietnam

October 19, 1970

Dear Jane,

They caught the guy who planted the bomb. It was a GI! I really have trouble accepting that, but it happened. A Vietnamese who worked on the base provided the device, and the GI placed it under the corner of the mess hall. I'm not happy with either the fact that one of our guys would do this or that the VC could have somebody working on our base.

Love,

Mike

SP4 Michael Ward

Fire Support Base Las Vegas

Republic of Vietnam

October 19, 1970

Dear Sean,

We know what happened now. The Vietnamese guy who burns the shit cans brought the bomb onto the base. But get this: one of the American cooks planted it. One of our own guys actually tried to kill some of us. Whoa! I've heard of officers being fragged in the infantry, but what was this about? Apparently, it involved some bullshit insults about the food that sent the cook berserk. "Berserk" is the word for it. The cook and the Vietnamese guy saw each other every day and hatched this plan together. Everyone is really shaken up by this, not just because of what did happen but also because of what could still happen.

If this Vietnamese guy, who was on base every day, was that quick to offer to provide a bomb, then he had to be a VC plant waiting for an opportunity. Were we just lucky when it finally came that his plan failed to work out? It reminds me of the kids waiting by the roadside. What else could be in store for us?

When I went to lunch today in our partially

repaired mess hall, it was very crowded and I ended up sitting with a couple of sergeants from the infantry platoon handling our perimeter security now. I asked how things were going, and one of them responded, "For you, war is hell; for us, it's a motherfucker."

As ever,

Mike

SP4 Michael Ward

Fire Support Base Las Vegas

Republic of Vietnam

October 22, 1970

Dear Jane,

There are racial problems in Vietnam, but I don't believe they're at the level they are in Germany. For one thing, we do not have to worry about discrimination in housing or restaurants. We all live in the same bunkers, and there are no bars or restaurants (at least anyplace that we go). There are quite a few black soldiers in our battery, two of them in FDC, and everyone gets along fine here. It doesn't even appear to be an issue. That does change when people are in the rear areas. On the bigger bases, whites tend to hang out with whites and blacks with blacks. Even before coming to Vietnam, I read an article that forward units don't have many racial problems because the soldiers count on each other for their personal safety, but tensions can arise in other places. The black soldiers here don't use the black power salute with each other, but sometimes they use it to greet black soldiers from other units who are passing through.

Please get back to me about Hawaii. That's where I'll be going anyway now, since that's where I put in for. I'd love to see your face, even for a minute!

I suspect that whatever you do with your holiday party, someone will find fault. All I can suggest is if you start with that understanding, you won't be disappointed by whatever happens. That's why they give that job to new people. The older people realize it's thankless. Before long, you'll be as safe from that assignment as they are.

Love,

Mike

SP4 Michael Ward

Fire Support Base Las Vegas

Republic of Vietnam

October 23, 1970

Dear Mom & Dad,

You had asked about my APO number. Even though our battery hasn't moved, our battalion headquarters has. As the troop withdrawal progresses, the army keeps moving our battalion headquarters closer and closer to division headquarters. It used to be out at LZ Bayonet. Now it's in Chu Lai. Since all our mail goes through battalion, our number changes accordingly, even though we are still in the same place.

I see that Governor Cahill is faced with the difficult task of informing his fellow Republican, President Nixon, that he cannot hold a rally at the Garden State Arts Center. The rules under which it was funded require that the facility be kept nonpolitical. I wonder what Agnew will have to say about that.

The Twenty-Fifth Infantry Division is being withdrawn from Vietnam. That's the one they sent me to by mistake in Cu Chi. What they're really sending back to the States, however, are the division colors. The soldiers who still have time left on their tours will finish them with other units, but they'll be taking places that otherwise would've been filled by replacements from the States. Vietnamization does seem to mean getting us out of here, but at the army's pace. I do wonder what will happen after that.

Maybe I shouldn't bother you with this, but I asked Jane to meet me in Hawaii for R&R. She hasn't given me an answer yet, but I'm getting the feeling that she either wants to see me at home or noplace on the face of the earth.

Love,

Mike

Chapter 8

REST
AND REJECTION

Mrs. Patrick Ward

Jersey City, New Jersey

October 23, 1970

Michael dear,

It's not a very nice day, overcast and rainy, but at least it isn't that cold. Went to dinner at The Alps last night with the Boyds. Your Uncle Peter and Aunt Patricia were there with some of their friends. At one point, the waitress came over and announced that the gentleman at the next table wanted to buy the "old bag" a drink. I told her that that was one of his nicer expressions.

St. Aloysius Church now has a new altar, which we saw last week. It's one where the priest faces the congregation. That part of Vatican II doesn't bother me, but I wish they'd bring back some of the old hymns.

The White House is categorically denying a rumor that it will order a unilateral cease-fire in Vietnam at the end of the month. What interests me more is how that rumor got started.

Lots of love,

Mom

SP4 Michael Ward

Fire Support Base Las Vegas

Republic of Vietnam

October 26, 1970

Dear Mom & Dad,

Well, we had quite a time with Typhoon Kate. I'm not sure what the difference is between a typhoon and a hurricane other than that the former is in the Pacific. Our FDC bunker was filling up with so much water that we had to stretch a hospital tent over it to keep operating. The radios had to be kept dry. Let me tell you, laying a hospital tent over a bunker in a typhoon is no easy task. We couldn't sleep in the FDC bunker, so we had to sleep in the fire direction officers' hooch, since it's above ground. Bunkers filled with water below ground level are not nice places to be.

Four days ago, I was surprised to be awarded the

Army Commendation Medal. Don't worry, it's not for any daring or courageous acts. "Meritorious achievement against hostile forces" is not the same thing as "valor." If you do your job well in a forward area, you're likely to receive such an award. A lot depends on where your unit is located. In our battalion, most of the people assigned to firebases eventually receive them.

I see they're publishing Ernest Hemingway's last work, *Islands in the Stream.* How many years after his death is it? When I get home, I'd like to read it. The last man to leave our battery had over thirty days cut from his tour. That's encouraging.

Love,

Mike

Jane O'Brien

Jersey City, New Jersey

October 30, 1970

Dear Michael,

The response to my request for three personal days was no, and it wasn't even a polite no. To tell the truth, I'm not even sure whether the reason was my being a newcomer or the fact that you're in Vietnam. "No, we're not going give someone who's been here less than a year time off to visit her soldier boyfriend." The strange thing is I understand they did allow just that last year for another teacher. So much has changed since Cambodia and Kent State. Well, at least if you're in Honolulu, I don't have to worry about the bar girls in Hong Kong or Bangkok.

Cindy Mitchell, who did the teachers' holiday party two years ago, has been helping me. She's familiar with the restaurants and their banquet menus. She just doesn't want to get the credit (a euphemism for the blame). This project is backing up my class prep work, however, so maybe there's some benefit from having Thanksgiving to catch up.

New Jersey is once again in the news for organized crime, maybe in a good way. Angelo Bruno was just sent away to prison, his first time. Apparently, he hasn't been convicted of any crime. Jeremy told me it's for contempt of court. Bruno was subpoenaed to testify before the New Jersey State Committee on Investigation, refused to do so, and ended up in jail for that refusal. This has been done with several organized crime figures. If they refuse to testify in front of the committee, they go to jail. If they do testify, they get bumped off by their cohorts. Interesting choice!

Love,

Jane

Mrs. Patrick Ward
Jersey City, New Jersey

November 1, 1970

Michael dear,

Another month out of the way! I'm getting a perverse joy from tearing pages off the calendar. We drove up from the shore today and are going to The Alps tonight for dinner. Tuesday is Election Day, so it's a holiday for your father but not for me. Catholic schools still don't give that off.

The weather down the shore was typical for this time of year. It was good for the trick-or-treaters yesterday. It may seem like an eternity for you, but it only seems like a couple of years to me when you were trick-or-treating. While I like to think back on those days, it's a little painful right now that you can't be here. I look forward to seeing my grandchildren in costume someday.

Lots of love,

Mom

Patrick Ward

Jersey City, New Jersey

November 2, 1970

Dear Mike,

While I have some time, I thought I'd dash off a letter. The stock market seems to be making a strong comeback after the big drop at the time of the

Cambodia invasion. It was at its lowest point since 1963. Apparently, investors now think the war is ending. I hope they're right.

Could I suggest you try to get a line off to your mother every few days? Even "Hello, it's a sunny day" would be enough. She gets very nervous when there's a gap in the letters. I realize it's often not you. We've had letters dated two days apart arrive ten days apart.

You missed quite a football game yesterday between the Giants and the Jets. The Giants were trailing 10–3 in the third quarter and then managed to score sixteen points in 114 seconds, starting with a safety when Jim Files tackled Chuck Mercein in the Jets' own end zone. The next rematch isn't until 1974, so the Jets have a long time to wait to get even, but at least you'll be able to watch that one. Almost sixty-four thousand fans attended the game at Shea Stadium.

Tomorrow is Election Day. The most publicized contest is for the United States Senate. Harrison Williams is running for reelection against Nelson Gross, the Republican state chairman. Williams seems to have a commanding lead, but some say he's a flip-flopper. They say under Johnson, he supported the Vietnam War, but once Nixon became president, he opposed it.

Affectionately,

Dad

SP4 Michael Ward

Fire Support Base Las Vegas

Republic of Vietnam

November 4, 1970

Dear Mom & Dad,

Well, Lt. Fitzsimmons has a baby son. He just got the word today and started handing us all cigars. The ones he gave out had blue rings on them saying "It's a boy." He was also prepared with ones that had pink rings saying "It's a girl." He's really flying high, but it must be hard being this far from home when your first child is born. He won't even get to see the baby for several months. He's very philosophical, though. He keeps saying it doesn't matter what this war does to us or to our own generation. All that matters is that the world is right for our children's generation.

Things are getting encouraging. Edwin Smart was supposed to go home January 10, but now he's been told he's leaving December 6 instead. I'll miss him. In addition to being a musician and cook, he's an excellent chess player. Sitting down at the chessboard with him is like taking a lesson. He's really looking forward to getting back to a piano. He hasn't been able to play for almost a year now.

Love,

Mike

Sean Ward

Jersey City, New Jersey

November 7, 1970

Hey Mike,

We've had a little rain today, not much, and it's not all that cold. The election results are all in now, and they don't look good for the Nixon-Agnew team. Nelson Gross suffered a big defeat in the Senate race against Harrison Williams, even in some heavily Republican counties like Monmouth and Bergen. It was not a good day for the Republican Party in the rest of the nation, either, but Nixon himself still seems to be popular.

Richard and I have been trying to get over to New York on the weekends now that summer's over. We found this new place called Pamela's Pub that has a nice twenties crowd. You'll like it when you get the chance. There'll be no more going down the shore for us, at least until springtime, and you could be home before then.

I haven't seen much of Jane lately. Maybe she's avoiding me. Are you guys arguing again? At least I'm not getting cross-examined on the contents of your letters.

Take care of yourself,

Sean

Mrs. Patrick Ward

Jersey City, New Jersey

November 9, 1970

Michael dear,

By the time you get this it will already be past Veterans Day, but let me wish you a happy one anyway. I ran into Charlie Fitzpatrick Saturday. He got back from Vietnam about a month ago and assures me you'll be home before long too because of all the reductions in the length of tours. He seemed a little off, absent-minded, like he wasn't quite sure where he was or what time of day it was. It might just take a little while for him to readjust. He wants to go to graduate business school, but the timing was bad for this semester. He plans on starting an MBA program at Rutgers in February.

I got in from school a little while ago. When I finish this letter, I'm going to walk down to Schimenti's to buy some food for dinner. One of the boys will then deliver it on his bicycle. It's so different here in the city from the shore, where people drive to the store and bring the groceries home in the car with them.

Lots of love,

Mom

SP4 Michael Ward

Fire Support Base Las Vegas

Republic of Vietnam

November 10, 1970

Dear Jane,

I received your letter. While I realize the decision wasn't yours to make, you don't seem really heartbroken about not seeing me, either. Nor did you even mention the possibility of a four-day weekend. Please let me know what's really on your mind. In August, you wrote that you wanted me to think of you as standing right beside me, and yet when the opportunity presents itself to do just that, your enthusiasm evaporates. There must be something more to this. Why don't you just tell me? Right now, I wouldn't mind running a holiday party, even if the price were too high and the food no good.

I had to go into Chu Lai the other day to pick up map coordinates they didn't want to transmit over the air. Our battalion headquarters and FDC are located there now. They keep moving them farther and farther back. We're the only ones who appear to be staying where we are.

Love,

Mike

SP4 Michael Ward

Fire Support Base Las Vegas

Republic of Vietnam

November 11, 1970

Dear Mom & Dad,

The secretary of the army recently announced that once our role here becomes completely advisory, the total strength of the entire army will drop to about 859,000, the lowest level since 1961. I would be happier if the discussion centered more around how to achieve that "completely advisory" role here in Vietnam rather than on how many fewer soldiers we'll need worldwide as a result.

There's been a lot of rain, rain, and more rain. At least we're not roasting the way we were before. Most of the guys leaving the battery now are going about 40 days before their scheduled DEROS dates, so I hope that keeps up.

It looks like Frank Sinatra is getting his way in Las Vegas. Doesn't he always? The district attorney who wanted him barred from working there because he didn't have a permit was defeated for reelection. The whole story seems convoluted to me, that some Caesar's Palace executive pulled a gun on Sinatra for complaining about a betting limit! There just has to be more to that story.

Love,

Mike

Patrick Ward

Jersey City, New Jersey

November 12, 1970

Dear Mike,

We had quite a to-do Tuesday at the law school. A radical student group tried to take over my classroom just as I was about to begin my Contracts class. They said they were going to use it for an antiwar meeting. My students were all there with their case books and had no intention of leaving. I had to get Dean Parker, who threatened the intruding students with expulsion and arrest if they didn't leave and permit the class to go forward. To everyone's relief, they finally did.

I do have a little trouble understanding the protesters. If they really wanted a place to meet, the school probably would have given them one that wasn't already in use. Why did they insist on trying to prevent other students who wanted to attend class from doing so? One of the reasons they backed down may have been that it became obvious they didn't have any support whatsoever from the regular students in the classroom, most of whom wanted nothing to do with them.

On a different note, the Giants have now won five games in a row with their 23–20 victory over the Dallas Cowboys on Sunday. Coach Alex Webster has even taken the unusual step of giving them an extra day off from practice in recognition. They may need the rest; they're playing the Washington Redskins next Sunday.

Affectionately,

Dad

Sean Ward

Jersey City, New Jersey

November 15, 1970

Hey Mike,

Let me first wish you a belated Veterans Day. Starting next year, you'll be able to celebrate the holiday annually. It started with the Armistice after World War I. We didn't enter that War until 1917. The armistice occurred on November 11 of 1918. They sure wrapped things up a lot faster there than we seem able to do in Vietnam!

We're going to Uncle Peter and Aunt Patricia's for Thanksgiving. It's time to give Mom a break. Every time an annual event occurs, she reminds us that you'll be here the next time we celebrate it.

Take care of yourself,

Sean

Mrs. Patrick Ward

Jersey City, New Jersey

November 15, 1970

Michael dear,

I hope this gets to you before you leave for Hawaii. Usually when people from New Jersey go there, they're traveling to a warmer climate. I'm not so sure that's true for you this time, but with the monsoon, maybe it is. I understand that the school board wouldn't give Jane the time off to join you. Don't be too harsh about it. It may be that she would rather be with you here than there, but she appears to be under a lot of strain herself. For her, this is where it's at. The public mood just isn't what it used to be when it comes to servicemen. Take comfort that she feels that your being here would be the solution.

Aunt Patricia is having us over for Thanksgiving. That means I don't have to cook a turkey this year! We may go to the shore next weekend but will stay up here for the holiday.

According to an article in the paper today, we have had 300,000 total casualties in Vietnam so far, 100,000 of them serious. From January 1965 through September 1970, 16,700 wounded have been transferred to the Veterans Administration, 2,000 with spinal cord injuries, 1,600 with major amputations, 220 blind, and 5,000 psychiatric cases. Enough is enough!

Lots of love,

Mom

SP4 Michael Ward

Fire Support Base Las Vegas

Republic of Vietnam

November 18, 1970

Dear Mom & Dad,

It's rained steadily for over two days now. I hope it lets up a little bit. As the troop withdrawals progress, we seem to be spreading out more. Two of our guns are now on a small LZ not too far from here. We still direct the fire for those guns, but we've had to set up an extra chart to do that. There are fewer guys here now, and the new ones coming into FDC haven't been trained for this job. Most of the guys who were here when I arrived in May had taken their AIT (advanced individual training) at Fort Sill in fire direction. The new ones all had just regular gun crew AIT, so I have to train them. It's really slowing down our response time. This is all part of the withdrawal. The other artillery battery has been pulled out of here already, so our battery commander is now also the commander of the firebase. Since we have fewer artillerymen here, there are supposed to be at least two infantry platoons with us at all times so the base is not undermanned.

That must have been quite some funeral service for President De Gaulle at Notre Dame Cathedral last week. He's being referred to as the greatest French leader since Napoleon. I see that Nixon was at the service and that there were additional services in Cairo,

Jerusalem, and even Bonn, West Germany. I wonder how most of the Germans feel. Hopefully their own anti-Nazi sentiment is running high enough now for them to look at de Gaulle positively.

On a lighter note, I see that the National Cash Register Company has developed an electronic substitute for bartenders. It's supposed to mix drinks faster than a human and even present the customer with a bill, but there's no indication what the invention's conversational skills are. Once I get home, I think I'll stick with a live bartender. I'd have trouble dealing with a machine on a bar.

Love,

Mike

Postcard

Hilton Hawaiian Village Hotel

Honolulu, Hawaii

November 24, 1970

Hi Jane,

Well, I'm here. Will be going back on Sunday. At least the beach is nice. I'll try not to drink too much. In any event, it's time away from Vietnam.

Biding my time,

Mike

Postcard

Hilton Hawaiian Village Hotel

Honolulu, Hawaii

November 25, 1970

Hi Mom & Dad,

Well, I'm in Honolulu. Went to the Polynesian Cultural Center today. Am enjoying the beach and planning on going to a luau.

Love,

Mike

Mrs. Patrick Ward

Jersey City, New Jersey

November 27, 1970

Michael dear,

Your phone call yesterday certainly made it a holiday for us. It was so wonderful just to hear your voice again. Hawaii is a much nicer place to be than Vietnam, even if you don't have the company you would have liked! You sounded so good, and it was even more encouraging to hear how much time is being cut off other soldiers' tours of duty.

It's hard to believe how warm it is today after how freezing it was on Tuesday. Dad says he doesn't plan on putting up a Christmas tree this year. He says he'll put it up when you come home, even if it's the wrong season. How will he get one? I hope he doesn't chop one down on someone's property.

Now that the election is over, some hotel association is advocating casino gambling in Atlantic City. I'm not in favor of the idea. I just like riding in a cart on the boardwalk with a blanket over me. I liked it even better when someone pushed the cart, as opposed to driving the ones with motors like they have now.

Lots of love,

Mom

SP4 Michael Ward

Fire Support Base Las Vegas

Republic of Vietnam

November 30, 1970

Dear Mom & Dad,

I'm back from R&R. It's still rainy here. While I was gone, another two guns were moved off this firebase to a small LZ, so we have only two guns left at this location. Our FDC is now doing the fire direction for all three locations. It was difficult cramming three separate charts into the limited space we have.

It's not just our guns that are spread out. The officers are, too. Capt. Berlen is the only artillery officer left on the base, and he's leaving to go home soon. Of course, the infantry who are handling our perimeter have their own officers. Since we don't have a fire direction officer anymore, I have to make sure all the firing data is ready to shoot before Capt. Berlen gets down here. He has to call the actual settings to the gun crews whether they're here or someplace else.

This is a big change in just the six months since I arrived. We used to have two full artillery batteries here, one of them with bigger guns, 155s. Now we have only a third of the guns of one battery, and I don't see the South Vietnamese coming forward with any type of replacement.

I don't have a lot of time now, but I wanted to let you know I was back safely.

Love,

Mike

Jane O'Brien

Jersey City, New Jersey

December 1, 1970

Dear Michael,

You know, you're right. Maybe my heart wasn't in Hawaii as much as you expected, but it's not because I don't care about you. It's because I'm still trying to figure out what you're doing there in the first place, not to mention why that should seriously interfere with the first real full-time job I've ever had. I still don't understand why you made the decision you did, but I have to live with it. I only ask that you extend me the same courtesy. You were no Andy Winberry yourself!

The young men who teach here with me admit that they're doing it only to avoid the draft. They believe that theirs is the moral choice. No, I'm not going to adopt that position, but it's all I hear every day. Jeremy, one of them, says it's what every intelligent man does. According to him, there are so many ways to avoid the draft, whether it's teaching, divinity school, Army Reserve, or questionable medical deferments, that the only men who do end up in the regular army either want to prove how tough they are or are just too dumb to know how to get out of it. I know you don't fit into either category, and I told him that. What I didn't tell him was how painful it was that even though you were neither stupid nor macho and had an easy alternative, you did what you did anyway, no matter what it did to our relationship.

Of more concern at this late point, there have been reports in the news that the Americal Division was using something called Agent Orange to defoliate the trees so the Viet Cong couldn't hide in them. It continued to use the chemical even after it was banned for health reasons by the Department of Defense. I hope you haven't been exposed! They say it can cause horrendous health problems. If you develop any symptoms, go to a doctor right away.

I'm sending you brownies. If they don't taste right, blame it on the fact that our stove must be the oldest stove in Jersey City. My baking skills may not be great, but I do the best I can. Even if they don't taste so good, I hope they remind you that everyone here, me included, is thinking of you. Who knows? Maybe they really will be delicious! Miracles do happen, even if they've been in short supply of late. I think I'm going to need one for this teachers' party, but I'm not going to bore you with that now.

Love,

Jane

Chapter 9
APATHY

Sgt. Michael Ward

Fire Support Base Las Vegas

Republic of Vietnam

December 1, 1970

Dear Mom & Dad,

I've been promoted. Now I'm a sergeant. At least I'll be making about $75 more a month now.

It's interesting to note how many positions that are supposed to be held by senior NCOs are now being held by guys of lower rank. Even as a sergeant, I'm well below the pay grade where a chief computer of a battery is supposed to be. Even our battalion operations sergeant is just a PFC. In the artillery, I think they're trying to fill these positions with college graduates who scored high on the math aptitude tests in lieu of seasoned NCOs, who are becoming scarce.

All the talk now is about how many guys are

going home early. People are leaving thirty or forty days before they were scheduled to. Part of the reason is so Nixon can get his forty thousand troops home by Christmas, which doesn't affect me. I am hoping, though, that some type of drop will still apply when my time draws short.

Love,

Mike

Sgt. Michael Ward

Fire Support Base Las Vegas

Republic of Vietnam

December 2, 1970

Dear Sean,

We had a visit from Military Intelligence yesterday. There were three of them. You can't tell their rank because they don't wear rank insignia. Instead they just have "US" on their lapels. I think that's more dangerous since it identifies them as MI, which would be of much more interest to the enemy. They were busy all day asking a lot of questions in FDC and looking at old fire missions. They stayed late, until after dark, and then wanted to leave.

Unfortunately, they had come by truck and planned to leave that way. I don't know what they were thinking. They insisted they couldn't stay overnight on a forward firebase. Whatever the risk of staying, it would be much less than the horrendous one of trying to drive that road after dark. I told them that, but they insisted on going. They asked for more ammunition, which I had to get from Capt. Berlen. He wouldn't even talk to them. He thought they were too stupid to bother with.

Five minutes after they left, they were back again, looking as pale as ghosts. They said the guard at the base entrance was dead with a bullet in his throat. He was! There was no further talk of their leaving at night. They stayed until this morning. I didn't know the guard; he was infantry, not artillery. I still feel bad for him, but even so, it's the first time I've seen some of the new guys take this war seriously.

Over the past few weeks, I've had a lot of opportunity to talk with Capt. Berlen. With our officers spread out the way they are, he's had to fill in a lot in FDC, and we have a lot of late-night talks. He's really worried about the attitude of some of the new arrivals and the lack of seasoned soldiers. The one-year tour of duty in Vietnam had always been a problem, since it takes time for soldiers to really learn their jobs. When the more experienced guys leave after ten and a half months, it's even worse. Capt. Berlen is going to have a long talk with the new commander. He said he made sure my promotion came through before he left so that I would be in a better position to keep some of the new guys on their toes.

As ever,

Mike

Mrs. Patrick Ward

Jersey City, New Jersey

December 4, 1970

Michael dear,

If this spring weather continues, nobody will need to go to Florida. It's not yet three thirty, and I'm already back from Amato's Seafood. We old-time Catholics will never get used to having anything else on Friday. Now I have to wait for the roof man.

I went shopping for your father at Barrett's yesterday. I wanted to get him some new shirts, if only he'll wear them. The place was jumping. There are lots of new styles that will look good on you after two years in green.

Betty McGill suggested to me that you should try to get an early out to go back to law school. Do you think if you registered for the spring semester the army would let you go? I can take care of things on this end, if you let me know.

Lots of love,

Mom

Sgt. Michael Ward

Fire Support Base Las Vegas

Republic of Vietnam

December 5, 1970

Dear Sean,

We had a close call the other day. One of our infantry companies called in a contact fire mission. "Contact" means they're receiving fire from the target, so it's important for us to take out that target quickly to stop the incoming fire. In this case, it was mortar fire coming from the opposite side of the infantry unit from our battery. That meant our projectiles had to pass over our infantry's heads to reach the target, the mortar tubes.

Unfortunately, the first round fell way short of the target. No one was hurt, but it scared the crap out of everyone. The reason it fell short was that the infantry unit was on a hill and the target was in a valley, so the altitude of the target was lower than the altitude of the observer. The quadrant elevation of the gun was set for the altitude of the target, which put the hill in the flight path of the projectile and made it hit the higher ground.

The only way to avoid this is to shoot the mission "high angle." The maximum range on a howitzer is achieved by setting the elevation of the tube at a 45-degree angle, what we call 800 mills. That range will decrease if the angle changes in either direction, up or down. Normally we fire at low angle, which means between 0 and 800 mills (0 to 45 degrees); the lower the angle, the shorter the distance the round travels. We can shoot the same distance by firing high angle, 800 to 1600 mills (45 to 90 degrees). In this case, however, the higher the angle, the shorter the distance. Low angle is generally more accurate, but high angle avoids obstacles better because by the time the projectile is near the target, it's coming almost straight down. It also provides better shrapnel dispersal.

If this mission had been fired high angle, it would have avoided the hill. Fortunately for us, decisions to fire high angle are generally not made at the battery level. There was no way to pass the blame on to us, but it still shook everybody up.

I've had to pick up another task as well. We have a large map of our AO (area of operations) on the wall that's covered with a hard sheet of plastic. The fire direction officer on the noon-to-midnight shift is responsible for marking the NDPs of the various infantry units on the plastic with grease pencil. He also has to mark the directions of any patrols to be sent out as well as the times each patrol would take place. Those grease pencil markings are considered the most security-sensitive data in our FDC. Since we have no fire direction officer now, I've been assigned that job. If I go off duty at midnight, I now get woken up in the middle of the night and asked if certain sectors are clear to shoot at or if we could have a patrol there. It's not fun deciphering grease pencil markings at three in the morning when you've been deep asleep.

As ever,

Mike

Sgt. Michael Ward

Fire Support Base Las Vegas

Republic of Vietnam

December 5, 1970

Dear Mom & Dad,

A new soldier arrived yesterday, an American Indian. His name is Leonard Beaver. He's a Seminole. When he told me that, I asked if he was from Florida. He acted real surprised and said, "No, Oklahoma." He acted even more surprised when I told him I thought the Seminoles were from Florida and asked me what I knew know about the Trail of Tears. I had no idea what he meant. He said in the first half of the nineteenth century, almost all American Indians living in the eastern states were forcibly removed to west of the Mississippi. How could I not have known that? I thought I knew American history. I'm glad he told me. I'll have to read more about it, but that's the type of thing that stays with you more after being explained by an Indian instead of a history book.

I'm going to have dinner now. We eat early here. After that I have a lot of data to work up, so I better get going.

Love,

Mike

Patrick Ward

Jersey City, New Jersey

December 6, 1970

Dear Mike,

I've been reading about a new program the military has to bring soldiers home from Vietnam for a two-week leave. In order to qualify, soldiers have to have been over there more than four but less than eight months. While that would ordinarily include you, there are some complications. The announcement was made only four days before the first flight left, which pretty much cut out soldiers in forward areas. Also, there was a photograph in the paper of men boarding a plane as part of this program. They all appeared to be considerably older than you or the average soldier. You probably had to be in the right place at the right time to benefit.

The Giants are playing the Buffalo Bills today. While they'll probably win this one, they'll have to win all three of their remaining games to qualify for the playoffs, and that's unlikely. The big news in New Jersey is that Walter Kidde & Company is donating nineteen acres of what had been industrial land to Essex County to use as a park. The tract in question has hundreds of dinosaur footprints considered to be among the most finely preserved and defined in the world.

Affectionately,

Dad

Sgt. Michael Ward

Fire Support Base Las Vegas

Republic of Vietnam

December 9, 1970

Dear Mom & Dad,

We had a change of command here the other day. Capt. Berlen is on his way back to Fort Sill for the Artillery Officer Advanced Course. I will miss him. He ran a tight ship, which was exactly what we needed both for our own safety and to protect the infantry with our fire support. Our new battery commander is a Capt. Edward Reynolds from Arizona.

Then today Jim Kallin left to go back to Chicago. He should be able to get a better martini there than he can here. I got another Commendation Medal yesterday, this one with Oak Leaf Cluster, which simply means it's not my first one. It's funny how I didn't get any medals for almost the first six months. Now I already have two. I'm not doing anything different. It's like everything changes once you've been in country for a while.

Apparently, NASA is doing everything it can to avoid a repeat of what happened to Apollo 13 in April. Even though the emergency landing was hailed as a spectacular success, they never made it to the moon. It would be better to avoid the problem in the first place. Alan Shepard, Stuart Roosa and Edgar Mitchell are scheduled to blast off January 31st, but there are already problems with the oxygen system and the computer, which have delayed testing. They say it will not delay the flight, but that shouldn't be the most important consideration.

Please put up at least a small Christmas tree even though I'm not there. On Christmas, I want to know there's a tree up in our home. It makes me feel better just knowing that our normal way of life is continuing.

Love,

Mike

Sgt. Michael Ward

Fire Support Base Las Vegas

Republic of Vietnam

December 10, 1970

Dear Jane,

I don't want to analyze your friend's moral beliefs. I guess it's none of my business, but he's completely wrong in his analysis of men here. There's no rah-rah.

We're not a sports team, and we don't act like one. What we are is cautious and subdued. We have to be. If we make the slightest error, we end up dropping a high-explosive round right on our own guys. When we do hit our target (which we couldn't do if we were stupid), it's not like scoring a touchdown. There are no fans and no cheerleaders. Those are all back home with the war protesters. Their form of moral commitment seems to have more perks than ours.

All of that notwithstanding, I have no quarrel with people who protest the war and want us to come home, but real war protesters don't wave Viet Cong flags at rallies. The people who do that aren't asking for peace; they're cheering on the other side. If communism is so wonderful, why did that sailor try to jump from a Soviet fishing vessel to a US Coast Guard cutter last week? The only people who seem to admire communism are the ones who don't have to live under its heel. Castro is so hard put to make it look good in Cuba he's had to change the calendar and move Christmas and New Year's Day to July to make it appear like he's meeting his sugar production quota

But why talk about anything else when I can thank you for those delicious brownies? They come out better on old stoves.

I know it hasn't been easy for you. Having a soldier for a boyfriend doesn't mean what it used to. But the way the drops have been going, I could be going home in early April instead of May. It'll be over then—not just the army, but also our being apart. No more deployments and no more training. I'll go back to law school, you'll have your teaching, and we'll both have each other, if that's what you still want. The things that have kept us apart won't be there anymore. We can let the rest of the world take care of itself. We don't have long to wait. Just say a little prayer.

Love,

Mike

Sgt. Michael Ward

Fire Support Base Las Vegas

Republic of Vietnam

December 11, 1971

Dear Sean,

When we came on duty at midnight, one of the new guys wasn't in the bunker. I won't bother with his name, but he didn't show up until a little after one o'clock, smelling like marijuana. I asked him where he'd been, and he said he'd been in one of the perimeter bunkers manned by the infantry. I told him if we received any fire missions during the next two hours, he was not to attempt to plot them on the charts, that I would cover that. I also told him if we did receive a mission, Capt. Reynolds would have to come, and he would notice his condition. He started whining "Ah shit, as if anyone really cares." I told him if he fucked up like this again, he'd find out exactly how much people here really cared.

Not only am I concerned about him, but I'm worried as hell about our perimeter security.

Carrying on,

Mike

Mrs. Patrick Ward

Jersey City, New Jersey

December 12, 1970

Michael dear,

You would not believe how many phone calls we've gotten in the last few days. *The Jersey Journal* ran an article on your recent medal. It was short, but everyone in Jersey City must have read it and are letting us know about it. I know you say this is a routine award, but still, be careful. Don't take any chances. You don't need any more medals. What you already have is more than enough.

The weather is not too good in New Jersey right now. We've had loads of rain and may get some snow. Upstate New York has already gotten eight inches of the white fluffy stuff.

The papers say Senator Case has been pushing a bill to prevent the president from entering into secret agreements with foreign countries. Why? As far as I'm concerned, he can make all the secret deals he wants as long as it ends the war and gets all of you home.

I hope the monsoon isn't too bad at your little firebase now. Soon it will be just a memory. Even the stuffed puppy you sent me is looking happier as the days count down.

Much love,

Mom

Patrick Ward

Jersey City, New Jersey

December 13, 1970

Dear Mike,

Have you started planning what you are going to do about law school? You will probably not get home in time to start the spring semester. What would you think about working at a law firm until September? Maybe you could even take summer courses at St. Peter's College. Did you know they have women students there now?

Speaking of education, President Nixon recently sent a letter to the chairman of the Commission on Campus Unrest. This quote from it is interesting from a rhetorical standpoint: "The new generation contains alienated young men of passion and idealism who march in protest against our efforts in Southeast Asia. It also contains young men of passion and idealism willing to risk their lives in an effort to rescue a hand-ful of comrades-in-arms in a North Vietnamese prison camp." It's a clever technique to make it look like he's trying to equate the two, while it's clear he is not. The repetition of "young men of passion and idealism" helps create the illusion that, on closer examination, is dispelled by comparing "march in protest against our efforts" with "willing to risk their lives in an effort to rescue."

We did not go down to the shore this weekend. The weather has been a little too cold to do anything.

Affectionately,

Dad

Sean Ward

Jersey City, New Jersey

December 15, 1970

Hey Mike,

Jack and Vivian gave a big party at their home Saturday. I didn't know most of the people there. I was talking for a while to a guy who'd been a captain in Vietnam up until eight months ago. He served in Military Intelligence and didn't seem all that reassur-ing. When I told him my brother was in the artil-lery and would be coming home soon, he just said, "Good—the sooner, the better!"

Why on earth are they blacking out the Super

Bowl in Florida? The game is going to be a sellout anyway. I understand the judge's ruling that there's no constitutional right to watch a football game on television, so maybe a lawsuit might not have been the best way to challenge it, but why is the NFL doing it? The traditional justification for blacking out televised football games, that local fans might not buy tickets if they can watch the game on television, doesn't apply at all when hordes of people are scrambling for any available seat.

Take care of yourself,

Sean

Sgt. Michael Ward

Fire Support Base Las Vegas

Republic of Vietnam

December 16, 1970

Dear Jane,

It will really be Christmas season in New Jersey by the time you receive this. We won't be going to midnight Mass together this year for the first time in three years. We won't be rushing back to my parents' afterwards to catch *A Christmas Carol* on TV, either. I like the way they always run that at one o'clock Christmas morning, probably to catch the people who are doing the same thing we do. Are you going to watch it anyway? A little bit of Scrooge and Bob Cratchit is good for everyone.

I've sent you something from PACEX. You should receive it in time. I'm sorry I can't hand it to you personally, but next year I can make up for that. How much time off do they give you for the holidays? Do you have any plans? With good luck, I might make it home for Easter, but I doubt it would be in time for spring break.

Well, back to plotting positions on the charts!

Love,

Mike

Jane O'Brien

Jersey City, New Jersey

December 19, 1970

Dear Michael,

The teachers' holiday party was last night at Bruno's, and guess who was the principal subject of conversation? You were! I never realized how much of a stir my being turned down for three days of leave has caused. Some of the older teachers and their husbands were ready to wring some necks. A few of them were World War II veterans, plus there was one Korean War veteran. The timing of the newspaper article about your last medal couldn't have been more critical. We almost had our own version of hard hats versus peace demonstrators, except that these were white-collar hard hats. In all the fuss, it seems I was immune to any criticism about the party preparation. I hope that doesn't mean they'll want me to do it again next year.

My parents hit me with a very big surprise Christmas present. They're taking me with them to Dublin during Christmas break. We are leaving December 26 and coming back January 2. I'm so excited! The thing I most want to do when I'm there is to visit Newgrange. That is the old passage tomb that's older than either Stonehenge or the pyramids in Egypt. It's a little outside Dublin but will make a nice day trip. I also want to see Kilmainham Gaol, where the leaders of the Easter Rising were incarcerated and executed in 1916. One of them, Joseph Plunkett, was married in the chapel right before he was shot by a firing squad. His wife was later imprisoned at the same jail, where she drew a now-famous picture of the Madonna and child on the wall of her cell.

Love,

Jane

Jim Kallin

Chicago, Illinois

December 20, 1970

Dear Mike,

I'm home now! At least I think so. My parents and

brothers and sisters were real happy to see me. Why do I feel they were the only ones? The rudeness to veterans we heard about, nobody's been like that, but no one's patting me on the back either. When I tell someone I just got back from Vietnam, they act sort of like I just got out of prison. They're not mean, but like they think you should be in drug rehab or something. I remember seeing the old magazine photos of the crowds welcoming World War II veterans home. Where did those people go?

Even the army wasn't much better. They didn't welcome us when we got off the bus from the air base at Fort Lewis. They had us line up and go around picking up trash off the ground. Should we expect civilians to be any better? The regulations require that when we get home this time of year, we should be issued overcoats to wear home. They tried to talk everyone out of taking one, though. They said they didn't have enough and that anyone asking for one might not get out of the army right away.

You thought you saw bad drugs in Chu Lai. Well, I'll tell you Cam Ranh Bay was much worse. There were even soldiers giving away heroin for free right in the barracks. They must have thought we were new guys they could get hooked. Why would they give it away to guys on their way home? Soldiers who deal drugs to other soldiers probably don't come from the top of the class. I stayed away from them.

Also, when you get to Fort Lewis, be sure to hide

your field jacket in your duffle bag. Ask them to give you one to wear there. You'll have to give it back when you leave, but they'll take whatever field jacket you're wearing anyway, even if it has your name and unit insignia on it. So make sure you have one of theirs to give back to them so they don't take yours.

Everything seems funny, though. I went to church on Sunday. Even though it was the same church I've been going to all my life, it felt like a different place. My bed doesn't even feel like my bed. Why don't I feel like I'm in my own room in my parents' house? I didn't think I'd have this much trouble readjusting. It's not like we're survivors of a platoon that was decimated. It must be even worse for those guys. I don't know any psychology, but there's a guy on my street who got back from Nam almost a year ago. He says that while we were there, our concept of reality changed without our even realizing it. When we get back to what used to be the norm for us, it all seems to be make-believe.

Let me tell you, though, if I live to be a hundred, the one thing I will never forget is the spontaneous cheer that went up in that plane once the landing wheels touched down on US soil. Up until then, everyone seemed like zombies after hours and hours of flight from Cam Ranh Bay to Okinawa to Japan and finally to Washington State, but once we realized we really were back, we just couldn't help ourselves. We went from near coma to chaos in the blink of an eye. Guys that wouldn't even talk to each other on the flight were slapping backs and hugging and crying. I've never seen so many emotions released at once.

Goodbye and good luck, and make it home safe, even if there won't be any ticker-tape parade to welcome you.

Stay well,

Jim

Sgt. Michael Ward

Fire Support Base Las Vegas

Republic of Vietnam

December 20, 1970

Dear Mom & Dad,

There weather here has been cool by Vietnam standards. We even had to put on our field jackets before sunrise a few times.

The political indictments in Hudson County are big news even over here. I just hope all of this litigation results in some long-term improvement.

I see that Aer Lingus had plans to start running flights between Vietnam and Korea, but the Irish Pilots Association forced them to be dropped. Its members weren't willing to fly that route. Even leaving the pilots' objections aside, why would an Irish airline want that flight segment anyway? It wouldn't be very likely to bring more tourism to the Emerald Isle.

You probably won't get this until after Christmas. I hope things have gone well for everyone. Next year will be much better.

Love,

Mike

Mrs. Patrick Ward

Jersey City, New Jersey

December 23, 1970

Michael dear,

Your father finally gave in and bought a small— and I mean *small*—Christmas tree. I don't think I'm going to need to bring down many boxes of ornaments from the attic, but I'll set up the nativity scene in the fireplace. It's the only thing we use the fireplace for. I guess in past generations someone must have had a fire there. We're going to put wreaths on the windows, so now you can dream about your lovely, cozy, properly decorated home in cold New Jersey.

I'm going to be fixing dinner here Christmas Day. Bill, Peggy and the kids are coming. I'll be doing a turkey, although frankly I like it better down the shore where you can buy the turkey from Hinck's already cooked.

We are missing you so much. This time of year has a way of bringing out those feelings, but we're going to see you, and it's going to be soon. I don't know why they aren't just bringing you all home now. Do they really think the result will be any different after these so-called peace talks in Paris? Anyway, Merry Christmas, dear!

Lots of love,

Mom

Sgt. Michael Ward

Fire Support Base Las Vegas

Republic of Vietnam

December 24, 1970

Dear Jane,

Happy Christmas Eve! Did you get the present I sent you yet? What are you doing for Christmas dinner? Are your parents having anyone over, or are you going to someone else's house?

The North Vietnamese have proclaimed a cease-fire for Christmas as of 1:00 a.m. today. Sometimes I think the only reason they do this is to move supplies and war materials without interference. The mess hall is planning some sort of holiday dinner tomorrow. I'm sure it won't be anything like home, but turkey, mashed potatoes, and gravy is something they should be able to pull off. It's not like asking for veal parmigiana. Santa Claus may have a little difficulty getting through, however. Maybe that's the real reason for the cease-fire!

You probably won't get this letter before January 1, so Happy New Year as well!

Love,

Mike

Sgt. Michael Ward

Fire Support Base Las Vegas

Republic of Vietnam

December 25, 1970

Dear Mom & Dad,

Well, today is Christmas Day, so Merry Christmas—and don't worry, we'll all be much merrier very soon. They are planning a nice dinner for us, at least what passes for a nice dinner here. Most of the guys I know have gone home by now. It's funny, but I feel like an old man. People keep asking me questions all the time about what we should be doing.

Despite the holidays, the big news around here is about Military Intelligence. Secretary Laird has directed that Defense Intelligence report directly to him without going through the Joint Chiefs of Staff. How can that possibly work? Can you really keep the Chiefs of Staff in the dark? More importantly, how does the secretary of defense get this valuable information back down to the operations level where it's needed? Is he again going to bypass the Chiefs of Staff by sending it directly to the field commanders affected by what's contained in the information? How will those field commanders respond if they need authorization from a higher command to act but the higher command is not privy to the same information? I hope there's some safeguard in place to cover this.

I keep looking out of the bunker for snowflakes, but a white Christmas here is highly improbable. I never realized one could actually miss snow. That might change the next time I have to pick up a snow shovel, however.

Love,

Mike

Sean Ward

Jersey City, New Jersey

December 27, 1970

Hey Mike,

We had a nice dinner here Christmas Day. Dad found some great champagne at the liquor store, and it went well with the turkey. He proposed a toast to you at the beginning of the dinner, but his voice wavered a little bit. He usually hides his emotions well.

The Christmas holidays seem different now than they did when we were in college. Back then it was all about coming home for a week and seeing your family and all your friends who went to different schools. Now it's just a day off with family and then back to work. I know it would seem different for you. The next time you come home will be a lot more important than Christmas vacation.

There was an article in the paper today about what appears to have been a very underhanded ploy by the North Vietnamese. They asked Senators Kennedy and Fulbright to send representatives to Paris to receive a new list of prisoners of war. Both senators complied, but when their envoys got there, all they were given was the same list that was previously released. This was particularly cruel since it had spiked the hopes of families of servicemen reported as missing in action, only to dash them when no new list was given. Why did they do this?

Take care of yourself,

Sean

Mrs. Patrick Ward

Jersey City, New Jersey

December 28, 1970

Michael dear,

We really, really missed you Christmas Day, especially at dinner. It was otherwise a lovely meal, though. Uncle Bill and Aunt Peggy were here with all the young ones in tow. No one was morose, so don't worry yourself. Everyone was just commenting how wonderful it's going to be in just a few short months.

I hope the army treated you nicely for Christmas, although it has its limits. When you get home, we'll have a real dinner and we'll drink champagne, which I don't think you'll get where you are now. I'll cook another turkey, but I don't think we'll bother with a tree. The one we have now is barely a token.

I read an article in the paper yesterday that a congressman from Mississippi went to Laos recently to meet with a North Vietnamese diplomat. He was assured that American prisoners of war were receiving special privileges for Christmas. This was reiterated in a Hanoi radio broadcast, which said a religious service was conducted. I pray this is true. Those poor families don't even know when their sons are coming home.

Lots of love,

Mom

Jane O'Brien

Jersey City, New Jersey

January 3, 1971

Dear Michael,

We returned from Ireland yesterday, and it was a wonderful trip. We got to both Newgrange and Kilmainham Gaol, which I mentioned to you, and also to Dublin Castle, the National Art Gallery, and Trinity College, where we saw the Book of Kells. Of course, we had some Guinness stout.

Tomorrow I return to school, and I'm looking forward to it. I can't show anyone pictures yet, but I can tell them about it. I'm sorry I didn't send any post-cards, but I never got a chance to sit down and write. Speaking of which, I don't have too much time right now with work tomorrow. Got to go.

Love always,

Jane

Sgt. Michael Ward

Fire Support Base Las Vegas

Republic of Vietnam

January 5, 1971

Dear Jane,

It's spooky how quiet it's been here lately. I guess I shouldn't complain, but I've been here long enough to know that the enemy sometimes does this deliberately to lull us into a false sense of security. I don't think it has that effect on the guys who've been here a long time. With us, the quieter it is, the more jumpy we become. But with all the rotation, there aren't as many of us around anymore, especially now that the army is cutting time off the ends of tours.

Thank you for your letter about the teachers' holiday party. You didn't say how you felt about the conflict, but I'm glad you were exempt from criticism. I read that the Nixon administration is planning on ending the draft in mid-1973. (I guess Nixon assumes he's getting reelected!) In addition to the regular army, they're hoping to rely on the Reserve and National Guard as their primary first responders. Of course, whether those components will still get the same number of enlistees without the draft as an incentive is problematic.

I'll be having breakfast in about an hour. We seem to be getting more real food for breakfast now. No powdered eggs! Let me know how your trip to Ireland went. I'd like to do that sometime. Would you mind going back?

I just picked this letter back up. Had to put it aside to take a radio call, nothing serious.

Love,

Mike

Mrs. Patrick Ward

Hudson City, New Jersey

January 5, 1971

Michael dear,

I was just reading that a former prisoner of war in North Vietnam is insisting the North Vietnamese are holding far more prisoners than they admit to. This man was released in August 1969 and was speaking at the United Nations. I really hope someone gets word to those poor families.

School has resumed. I just got back about an hour ago. Your father will still be a little while. We did get your letter dated Christmas Day, and we will be very merry very soon. I'm fixing a little liver and bacon for dinner tonight. You know how much your father likes that, and you too. I just called Schimenti's Market, so it should be delivered soon.

Lots of love,

Mom

Patrick Ward

Jersey City, New Jersey

January 8, 1971

Dear Mike,

I'm spending most of my time now getting ready for the new semester. I'll be teaching two sections of Contracts and one of Commercial Law II. I've taught them both before. Contract law doesn't change very much, at least the common law part that we teach first-year students. I know you have already had that. Commercial Law II is somewhat flexible, since there are always new developments in secured transactions. That will require more preparation on my part to stay current.

Your mother and I might take a ride down the shore before classes begin just to check on the house.

The golf club is closed for January, so we can't have dinner there. We may eat at Pals Aweigh.

For as much as we have all come to realize that these are troubling times and come to expect, if not accept, some very bizarre behavior, I still cannot absorb the reports that someone actually firebombed the headquarters of the Camp Fire Girls in Pomona, California. It just leaves me confounded and incredulous. In the meantime, you just stay very cautious where you are.

Affectionately,

Dad

Sgt. Michael Ward

Fire Support Base Las Vegas

Republic of Vietnam

January 12, 1971

Dear Mom & Dad,

I was just reading an article that said in the first ten and a half months of 1970, there were just over seven hundred hospital visits in Vietnam related to illegal drug use. That made me think. The press has estimated that illegal drug use in Vietnam involves over seventy-five percent of the troops. We probably had a daily average of four hundred thousand servicemen here during the time frame reported. If that estimate is correct, it would mean about three hundred thousand were using illegal drugs and only about seven hundred hospital visits! Please! Any city hospital back in the United States could tell them that a lot more than one out of every 428 illegal drug users ends up in the hospital, especially where heroin is one of the drugs. I don't doubt that there is significant drug use in some rear areas, but reports of it at forward locations are blown way out of proportion.

We had shrimp for lunch today with watermelon for dessert, a nice change. I've been reading *QB VII* by Leon Uris. While it's a novel about a libel lawsuit by a former concentration camp doctor against an author, it was apparently inspired by an actual lawsuit against Uris himself.

Love,

Mike

Sgt. Michael Ward

Fire Support Base Las Vegas

Republic of Vietnam

January 12, 1971

Dear Jane,

According to the Pentagon, the role of US forces here in Vietnam will be curtailed as of May 1. The combat troops that remain will concentrate on providing air and artillery support to the South Vietnamese, as well as security. It may have been better if we had done just that from the start. The ARVN knew the countryside and spoke the language, neither of which we did. Why did our troops have to take over the bulk of the field operations? I guess there's no use complaining about it now, but sometimes I feel that this was some giant fiasco.

There's nothing wrong with defending one country from a takeover by another, but there has to be some real plan in place for how to do it. Simply counting bodies doesn't work. Also the government we support has to be viable. I'm not happy with the present South Vietnamese government, but the problem is not (as some war protesters claim) that they're a puppet of the US. It's just the opposite. The fact of the matter is the South Vietnamese government is not very cooperative with us at all. I hope I'm not boring you with this.

The weather has been improving. At least our bunker is dry now.

Love,

Mike

Mrs. Patrick Ward

Jersey City, New Jersey

January 13, 1971

Michael dear,

It's a good thing you have plans to go back to law school. The nation's businesses aren't stepping up to the plate to hire vets the way they did after World War II. Not only is unemployment higher among veterans than non-veterans, but veterans who do get jobs usually end up with the lowest-level positions. The better jobs have already been taken by people who avoided service and got hired before the job market got so tight. All the same, we are very much looking forward to your coming home to a not-so-grateful nation.

It's very, very cold today. The high temperature is still in the twenties. I'm cooking a leg of lamb tonight in the oven, with roast potatoes and carrots in the same pan. I'll be fixing some of that for you soon.

Lots of love,

Mom

Sgt. Michael Ward

Fire Support Base Las Vegas

Republic of Vietnam

January 15, 1971

Dear Mom & Dad,

Well, after being here almost eight months, I finally got to see some Donut Dollies. I had heard about them for a long time. They're the young female Red Cross volunteers who come to Vietnam to entertain the servicemen. I'm not sure exactly how they go about this. Maybe it's just by handing out donuts and smiling. Anyway, I've never seen any of them before.

They're usually on the big bases like Chu Lai, and the few times I was there, I didn't have a lot of time for those things. They do fly out to firebases by helicopter occasionally, but we (the guys in FDC) are usually on duty then or sleeping from being up the whole night before.

Yesterday, however, we were working in our bunker and they were in the mess hall with the gun crews, having donuts I guess. We got a radio call that one of our infantry companies had run into a daytime ambush and needed supporting artillery fire to break out of it. The siren went off to alert the crews to man the guns. I'm not sure what the dollies must have thought when they heard the siren and all the men rushed out of the mess hall. In any event, as we were working up the gun settings, four of them filed into the FDC bunker, escorted by an officer none of us recognized. They looked around for a while and really seemed to be interested in what was happening. After about fifteen minutes, however, they left. We were so completely absorbed by the fire mission that we didn't even get to speak with them. My one and only encounter with the Donut Dollies didn't even result in saying hello!

Love,

Mike

Sgt. Michael Ward

Fire Support Base Las Vegas

Republic of Vietnam

January 16, 1971

Dear Sean,

I'm not too keen on how things are going here at the firebase. We're not getting any new guys in that have been trained in fire direction. The first sergeant is selecting men from the gun crews he thinks can handle it and then telling me to train them. I'm doing the best I can, but it's hard to train someone when the only missions we have to work up are real ones where people can get killed. At Fort Sill, we practiced working up fire missions all the time. No shots were fired. The instructor just wanted to teach us to do the numbers correctly, and we could experiment by trial and error without causing any harm. I've asked Lt. Miller, our new fire direction officer (yes, we finally got one), if we can do practice missions here, and the only response I got was "Hmph!" I really miss Lt. Fitzsimmons, but at least he's finally getting to see his son.

I'm beginning to realize why I was so confused when I first arrived in Vietnam about what the Twenty-Third Infantry Division was. Apparently, the army has directed the phasing out of the denomination "Americal Division." It's supposedly because of the bad press about My Lai. The Americal Division has always had the numerical designation of the Twenty-Third Infantry Division, but in the past, the practice was not to use it. Now they think that avoiding the term Americal will somehow disassociate us! I was truly shocked by what happened in My Lai, but that was almost three years ago when none of us were here. I realize that legal proceedings have to be conducted, but it's not making things easy for us today when we don't do things like that. We weren't even allowed to shoot at a large group of apparent soldiers on Batangan Peninsula simply because the observer was too far away to see their weapons. We may never know the real story about why My Lai happened, but it casts a long shadow.

As ever,

Mike

Jane O'Brien

Jersey City, New Jersey

January 17, 1971

Dear Michael,

The big news in New Jersey teaching now has nothing to do with our board of education but more with the state board of higher education, which recently revoked the academic accreditation of a fundamentalist Christian college in Cape May. The reasons given included the lack of sufficient graduate degrees by its faculty and the fact that some of the courses listed in its catalog don't really exist. The reverend who runs the school says the whole thing is a "liberal frame-up."

I bought Janis Joplin's posthumous album yesterday. Columbia Records just released it last week. It's called *Pearl* and is becoming a big hit, especially one song called "Me and Bobby McGee."

I'm going to Judy Durkin's wedding next Saturday. I hope you don't mind, but I asked Jeremy to accompany me. It's not like we're dating or anything, but I'm nervous about going alone since I don't know Judy's friends from college at all and don't want to stand around looking silly with no one to talk to.

We're into the exam correcting period in school now—fortunately, not very difficult in third grade. The new semester starts next week. Hooray, I will have made it through one whole semester without screwing up anything badly, not even the holiday party.

Love always,

Jane

Chapter 10
ESCORT

Sgt. Michael Ward

Fire Support Base Las Vegas

Republic of Vietnam

January 19, 1971

Dear Mom & Dad,

I read in *Stars and Stripes* that a US Army sergeant recently tried to bring his Vietnamese wife and two-month-old daughter to the United States. No South Vietnamese officials would process his request without being paid off. The baby's birth certificate cost him $480. His wife's cost him $400. He had to pay $500 for a background report and $340 for a permit for his wife to accompany him to Saigon. The sergeant in question had recently been back to the United States to attend the funeral of his brother, a Specialist 4 who had been killed in Vietnam.

Is this the government Americans are risking their

lives to defend? Is this the government his brother died to defend? Senator Griffin of Michigan has intervened and is making sure the family gets here. The South Vietnamese Embassy has denied that this happened.

Love,

Mike

Sgt. Michael Ward

Fire Support Base Las Vegas

Republic of Vietnam

January 20, 1971

Dear Jane,

When I first got here, the thing I missed most was seasoned food. Now I dream about being able to put on clean, dry socks in the morning. The days are counting down, though, and it won't be long. I think the first thing I'll do when I get back is to go out and buy a whole drawerful of new socks. That and take a hot bath. After that, we can get some Italian food. How about calamari marinara over linguini and some red wine?

In addition to Ireland, I think we should go to Egypt someday. What got me on to that were the news reports about finding jewels in the bodies of the mummies themselves. People used to think that except for what was found in King Tutankhamen's tomb, all the jewelry of the pharaohs had been stolen by ancient grave robbers. Then just recently, they X-rayed some of the mummies and found numerous concealed valuables. I guess the thieves stayed away from the bodies. We're not likely to discover any new tombs, but we could get our picture taken on a camel in front of the Sphinx.

The weather has been miserable here lately, but it should be getting better soon. The monsoon north of the central highlands is different than it is in the south.

Love,

Mike

Mrs. Patrick Ward

Jersey City, New Jersey

January 22, 1971

Michael dear,

Father Daniel Berrigan tape-recorded a message in prison recently that was sent to the radical group, the Weathermen, urging them to forsake violence as a mode of operation. In it he says, "No principle is worth the sacrifice of a single human being." Up to that point, he sounds compassionate and would probably draw considerable sympathy. Later, though, he is reported to have said that the Viet Cong should not have this restraint imposed on them. He just lost the empathy of a lot of mothers.

There is a little mix of snow and rain today, not much. I got home from school about an hour ago and am going to head out to Amato's to buy some dinner. I'll try to be home by the time your father gets back. There will be no trip to Sea Girt this weekend.

I'm happy they at least seem to feed you well at your little base. Even if the food is a little boring, you don't have to worry about getting sick or malnourished, and you're going to have some nice meals once you get home. I better get going to my food shopping.

Lots of love,

Mom

Sgt. Michael Ward

Fire Support Base Las Vegas

Republic of Vietnam

January 23, 1971

Dear Sean,

It got bad with Lt. Miller yesterday. I tried to press him more about doing practice missions. I pointed out that our time lapsed from receipt of call to first shot out had increased from four minutes to eight minutes. I said that a four-minute delay could cost infantrymen their lives. He seemed to coil and strike. "And what would you know about that? I spent six fucking months out there watching what was happening while you were living in a bunker." Then he collapsed like a pile of laundry.

Doug and I helped him into a chair. He was really shaking and saying, "None of that shit matters anymore; we're done here." All he does now is sit and stare straight ahead. I've had to call the firing data up to the guns, but no one's complaining. There seems to be a general understanding that everyone is trying to make do with whatever works.

I did ask one of the infantry lieutenants about drug use. He said it's as much as they can do to keep everyone drug-free in the field. They don't want them setting off any land mines. On the firebase, though, they ease up. I hope not so much that they can't watch the perimeter.

See you soon,

Mike

Sgt. Michael Ward

Fire Support Base Las Vegas

Republic of Vietnam

January 27, 1971

Dear Mom & Dad,

I heard the American ambassador to the Republic of Vietnam says the pacification program here has been so successful that the term pacification has become outmoded. Now he said we need to "consolidate territorial security gains." To what territorial security gains is he referring, exactly? I don't know of any. Do you think he could be a little more specific as to where these gains have taken place? I won't hold my breath waiting for that.

In a little while, we will start receiving the infantry NDPs and start calculating the defensive targets. It gets dark early this time of year, so we have to shoot them in a little sooner while the forward observer can still see his surroundings. In any event, I better close and get busy.

Love,

Mike

Sean Ward

Jersey City, New Jersey

January 27, 1971

Hey Mike,

The holidays are over, and the Super Bowl too. The game was exciting, with the winning field goal kicked with only five seconds to go. Since neither the Giants nor the Jets were involved, I guess I'm sort of happy for Baltimore.

Richard went to Judy Durkin's wedding on Saturday. He said he saw Jane there. She had some guy named Jeremy with her and didn't dance with anyone else. Richard asked her, but she said, "Not right now." I don't know how things are with you and her.

Is it possible that you could be coming home in just two months? If they knock forty days off your tour, that would be about right. Although I worry about you, I worry about Mom more. I know she always tries to confine her comments to light subjects like parties and dinners, but that's only to conceal the fact that she's hurting. I'm sure you realize it's harder for her because of losing Uncle Phil in World War II. He was supposed to be in a safe area when he was killed. Since she moved back to live with Gram when Dad was in the navy, she still remembers the parish priest arriving with the marine captain to give them the news. *Stay alert now more than ever!* I know I don't need to tell you that you don't have enough of your own guys there anymore.

Take care of yourself,

Sean

Sgt. Michael Ward

Fire Support Base Las Vegas

Republic of Vietnam

January 29, 1971

Dear Jane,

It's about a quarter after five, and we just finished eating dinner. When we're on duty like this, we go over to the mess hall one at a time and bring the food back here to eat. That way, there are always enough of us here to work up firing data if we get an emergency call. They sound a siren when that happens, so everyone runs out of the mess hall anyway. The gun crews have to get to their gun pits right away. When the call comes into the FDC, the FADAC operator has to take a quick look at a vertical chart and give an approximate azimuth. For example, if we were to fire generally south, that would be 3,200 mills (180 degrees in civilian terminology). Then the fire direction officer calls over the loudspeaker, "Battery adjust three-two-hundred, battery adjust three-two hundred." That's when they sound the siren. That didn't happen today, though. We just came back and ate our dinner.

I don't mind your taking someone to a wedding As I said before I left, I don't expect your life to come to a standstill just because I'm over here. You should go to the wedding, and I can certainly understand your wanting an escort. The same name does seem to pop up an awful lot, though.

Love,

Mike

Jane O'Brien

Jersey City, New Jersey

January 29, 1971

Dear Michael,

We're two weeks into the new semester now, and things seem to be off to a good start. The principal is polite, almost gracious, and (amazingly!) the other teachers are all friendly at this point. Now, if the pupils would just behave.

Speaking of behaving, there was a big article in last week's Sunday *Times* about drug use in Vietnam, about how officers are embarrassed when they catch soldiers doing drugs because they know since it's so widespread there's nothing they can do about it. What's the story on this? Do you know more than you're telling me? Please let me know if everything is all right.

One of the other single teachers, Pamela Hofstadter, is having a small party tonight, so I'm going over there for a little while. It's awfully cold out, so I'll have to bundle up, but at least there's no snow.

Love always,

Jane

Mrs. Patrick Ward

Jersey City, New Jersey

February 1, 1971

Michael dear,

I'm back at school today. We've had a tiny amount

of snow, nothing to write home about—but then, I'm not writing home. I'm writing to Vietnam, where snow might sound like fun. We had decent weather down the shore this weekend—decent for January, that is, if a little windy. The Wallaces popped in last evening and joined us for dinner at Pals Aweigh. We really had a hilarious evening, everyone being in a party mood. They were absolutely delighted that you would be coming home soon.

What is going on with Vice President Agnew and Congressman Andrews? Agnew is claiming Andrews made some bad comments about the FBI's handling of the Berrigan brother priests. Andrews agreed he'd deserve criticism if he had made those remarks, but he says he never said any such thing. I'm sure Agnew will have something more to say.

There was also much discussion of Joe and Cathy's upcoming wedding. It looks like it's going to be quite an affair. It's too bad you won't be home for that. What do they say about those wedding bells?

I can't believe I read a letter in the *Times* today from a minister who said that while he had sympathy for the families of American POWs in North Vietnam, he was growing impatient with their attempts to persuade Hanoi to release the prisoners. He's growing impatient with them! Is that so? A clergyman, no less! I wonder if he can even begin to comprehend how much *their* patience has been tried.

On a more positive note, the University of

Massachusetts is starting a new program to recruit Vietnam veterans for its student body. It's refreshing to see someone planning to help veterans by providing them with better education rather than suggesting what you all need is drug rehabilitation and psychiatric care.

Lots of love,

Mom

Sgt. Michael Ward

Fire Support Base Las Vegas

Republic of Vietnam

February 4, 1971

Dear Mom & Dad,

The monsoon has been winding down. We still get some rain, but nothing like before. We're able to sleep in our bunker now without any problem. It looks like things are beginning to heat up in, of all places, Saigon. The guys there aren't used to that. Just over the past ten days, there have been two terrorist bombs set off downtown, both of them in theaters. The most recent, on Friday, blew a hole in the American bachelor officers' quarters next door. If they can't even keep Saigon peaceful, how are they going to control the countryside?

On a less militaristic note, I read that Barbra Streisand recently paid a visit to the Canadian House of Commons. Apparently, she and Prime Minister

Trudeau have something going. One member of the opposition party asked Trudeau to keep his eyes off the visitors' gallery long enough to answer a question.

It looks like Apollo 14 is off the ground. Let's just hope it makes it to the moon, unlike Apollo 13.

Eddie Dolan, our generator operator, just got his orders to go home today, thirty-seven days early. He'll be leaving the firebase Monday.

Love,

Mike

Sgt. Michael Ward

Fire Support Base Las Vegas

Republic of Vietnam

February 7, 1971

Dear Jane,

If there is one thing you don't have to worry about at all, it's my getting involved with drugs. For one thing, I'm not that stupid, but for another, they aren't nearly as widespread in areas like this as they are on the major bases in the rear. We don't even have our own bunks. We have to take turns sleeping. We're never alone. No one could use drugs without someone seeing it.

I'll not go so far as to say there's no drug use here. There are some infantrymen who use drugs on a firebase, even if they won't use them in the field. As

I told Sean, I believe some of our guys use drugs in the infantry bunkers. They could never do it in our cramped quarters. The officers and NCOs we have here wouldn't turn a blind eye, especially considering how critical our gun settings are. I did see serious drugs when I was in Chu Lai, and I know that they're widespread in Cam Ranh Bay also. Maybe that's how officers act there. I don't know, but there are a lot more news reporters in those places, and they seem to be the ones who spread these stories.

All of that aside, how are you really doing? Are you all that worried about these things, or is there something else? Let me know if there's anything I can do. It won't be long before I will be there.

Love,

Mike

Mrs. Patrick Ward

Jersey City, New Jersey

February 8, 1971

Michael dear,

I spent most of my weekend getting your room reorganized. It started me thinking. It looks just the same now as it did when you graduated from high school. Do you think as a twenty-four-year-old veteran you might want something different? Have you outgrown the college pennants? How about framing the citations that came with your medals and hanging them on the wall? You could probably use new wallpaper, too. What you have now was what was put up when you were in grammar school. It really makes me feel good to think about these things.

It's raining today. Of course, it's nothing like you had recently! It's not cold enough to turn to snow, but freezing rain can feel worse. By the time you get here, we should be out of these conditions.

Lots of love,

Mom

Sgt. Michael Ward

Fire Support Base Las Vegas

Republic of Vietnam

February 10, 1971

Dear Sean,

I'm no military strategist, but I can't see how anyone could really believe we're making any progress here. We keep sending infantry units into the same areas over and over again, recapturing the same ground, only to abandon it back to the same enemy and let the North Vietnamese move back in again and again and again. I've been here nine fucking months now, and we're no closer to accomplishing anything than we were when I stepped off the plane.

It's actually been almost seven years since the Gulf of Tonkin, which I count as the beginning of the war. (I know we've been here longer.) Seven years after Pearl Harbor was December '48, and World War II had been over for three years. There was no one-year period of losing lives while making no progress. Every year, they kept getting closer to Berlin or Tokyo. I would think a West Point freshman could easily point this out to the Joint Chiefs of Staff.

Enough of that! We'll be having breakfast in about an hour at 6:30. There was a visit from an officer named Maj. Barnaby yesterday that resulted in some unusual exercises. We had to figure out how to shoot "propaganda rounds." Really! When the shell is over the target, it pops open and drops leaflets onto the enemy troops. I'm not kidding!

The rounds themselves are left over from World War II. My first reaction was what good are flyers that say "der Fuhrer schtinks"? We were then told that the projectiles themselves are empty, and the papers are put in them right before loading. The first few times we fired them, the leaflets didn't fall out. Then one of the older sergeants asked the gun crew if they were taking a wooden block out of the shell before putting the flyers in. They told him they were. He said they should leave the wooden block in the shell and pack the sheets of paper around it. They did that on the next round, and the flyers fluttered to the ground perfectly. I couldn't help but think this might have made sense five years ago, but what can it possibly accomplish at this point?

What we're waiting for now is for one of our infantry companies to be attacked so we can respond with leaflets rather than high explosives! They'll love that!

I had to work up all the details with the major. Lt. Miller just sat in the chair staring at the wall. Maj. Barnaby apparently sensed something was wrong and didn't even attempt to speak with him. Miller comes to the FDC and goes every day, but that's all he does. I've taken advantage of his near coma to do some practice missions quietly, so as not to set him off again. He doesn't seem to notice, though. I've also made sure everyone's magazines are loaded. All of the men are issued two bandoliers of eight magazines each when they arrive. It amazes me that most of the new guys never bothered to load their magazines with ammunition. It takes time—certainly too much time to do in the middle of a sapper attack. I've also insisted that all helmets and flak jackets be hung near the door next to the rifle rack, so they can be grabbed quickly. Considering the condition of our perimeter security, which we can't do anything about, we need to beef up the security of our own bunker. Some of the guys think this is a waste of time. I hope they're right.

As ever,

Mike

Patrick Ward
Jersey City, New Jersey

February 11, 1971

Dear Mike,

The new inductees to the Football Hall of Fame this year will include Vince Lombardi, Andy Robustelli, and Y. A. Tittle. Their formal induction will take place July 31 in Canton, Ohio. Apparently, the rule that requires players to be retired for five years before they are eligible does not apply to Lombardi, since he was a coach and never a player. Jim Brown, who was also selected, just barely made the five years.

You might want to exercise a little extra caution. I read that combat activity in South Vietnam is at the highest level that it has been in ten months. This is the opposite of what we have been hearing for some time now. This would be consistent with what is being said about the Paris peace talks. The only card that the US has to play anymore is Vietnamization, and unless the North Vietnamese believe the South Vietnamese can handle them on their own, they have no need to compromise. The whole diplomatic scenario gives the appearance of a smoke screen where we are pretending to negotiate a settlement, when in fact all we are doing is withdrawing. This recent surge of attacks further suggests the North Vietnamese are not, as some people believe, necessarily going to wait for the Americans to be completely out of there before they make their move. Be careful and keep your eyes open.

Affectionately,

Dad

Jane O'Brien

Jersey City, New Jersey

February 12, 1971

Dear Michael,

I didn't want to tell you because I didn't want to worry you, but I found a lump in my breast last week. No, you don't need to worry now. I went to the doctor yesterday and had it aspirated. It was just a cyst. It had me so upset I couldn't even drive myself to the doctor's office. I had to get Jeremy to take me after school yesterday. The answer to the question you haven't asked is no, we're not dating. But who else do I have to count on? You're not here and haven't been for almost two years. Beth and Angela don't get off work until five o'clock, so it had to be a teacher who got off at three! I didn't even tell my parents, since they would have been worse than I was.

Tomorrow starts a three-day weekend, Lincoln's Birthday. I'm not planning anything other than calming down. A gang of teachers is going to the movies tomorrow. We're going to see *The First Time* with Jacqueline Bisset. Oh, and happy Valentine's Day!

Love always,

Jane

Chapter 11
THREE'S A CROWD

Sgt. Michael Ward

Fire Support Base Las Vegas

Republic of Vietnam

February 12, 1971

Dear Jane,

Happy Lincoln's Birthday! We don't celebrate it much here. Of course, it's not a national holiday, only a state holiday in the northern states like New Jersey. I was talking with one of the new men who arrived this week who's from Puerto Rico. They're subject to the draft there, too. His name is Luis Salazar. He's very interesting to talk to. He was telling me that in his hometown, when a young man wants to impress a young lady, he and all his friends gather outside her window. They play guitars, and he sings to her. I thought of trying that with you, but I don't have any friends who play guitars. Also, in Jersey City, someone would probably call the police if we gathered outside your house and made any kind of noise.

Love,

Mike

Mrs. Patrick Ward

Jersey City, New Jersey

February 15, 1971

Michael dear,

Did you know the United States has to be ready to fight one and a half wars? I figured you and your friends should be the first to hear about this. In reality, you would usually be the last. The secretary of defense says despite the withdrawal from Vietnam, he needs an increase in the budget for his department. Silly me to think the opposite! In any event, the Nixon administration recently announced that the United States must remain fully prepared to engage in one and one-half wars and will need more money for this purpose.

How exactly does one go about fighting half a war? Is one side at war and the other side at peace? Isn't that like trying to clap one hand? Maybe the one war and the half-war would both be in the same place. Would that be the case if one country were at war with two countries at the same location? Are you involved in one and a half wars, or is Vietnam now just half a war? It seems to me the administration is engaging in a lot of semantic nonsense to try to avoid cutting its defense budget as part of the withdrawal from Vietnam and, at this point, I don't really care—as long as they get you out of there!

Lots of love,

Mom

Sean Ward

Jersey City, New Jersey

February 15, 1971

Hey Mike,

I don't know what your take is on Laos. For myself, however, even if an argument could have been made for Cambodia, Laos is much more of a stretch. If nothing else, our troop strength is much lower now. We're hoping (realistically?) that South Vietnam can pick up the slack and, at the same time, throwing them into a major operation we would have difficulty executing even if we still had our full troop strength. Their mission is something like that of the German U-boats in World War II. No matter how many freighters and tankers they sank, enough were going to get through to keep the British supplied. They just couldn't counteract the force of American industrial production.

On the other hand, what we're dealing with here is the flip side of that. Britain had to supply a very big war machine; the North Vietnamese can operate on a shoestring. One way or another, they're always going to get the minimal supplies they need through. What we're trying to get the South Vietnamese to do is the functional equivalent of having a group of soldiers running around a field with umbrellas trying to keep rain from hitting the ground.

Listen to me—for all my supposed military expertise, you'd think they would call me up for active duty.

Around here, things are kind of quiet. Well, it's February. Not just that, but in the almost two years you've been gone, most of our friends have gotten married. The old gang just isn't there anymore, neither the guys nor the gals. When you get back, you may have to find a whole new circle of friends.

Not to throw fuel on the fire, but Richard went to the war protest at Times Square Tuesday. He saw Jane there with the same guy she was with at the wedding. She was very enthusiastic during the outburst against the Laos invasion, but when the crowd started chanting "Ho, Ho, Ho Chi Minh," she just stared down at her shoes and kept her mouth shut. The guy (is his name Jeremy?) nudged her with the heel of his hand. She didn't look up or say anything, but she did put her arm around his waist. I'm sorry, but I didn't want to keep this from you.

Take care of yourself,

Sean

Sgt. Michael Ward

Fire Support Base Las Vegas

Republic of Vietnam

February 16, 1971

Dear Mom & Dad,

It's time to go home. When I first came here, I felt that while the situation was awful, we were doing the right thing. The north wanted to take over the south. The south didn't want to be taken over by the north. Even leaving the communist versus capitalist thing aside, we were defending a country under attack. I still think most of the South Vietnamese people feel that way, but they've given up, and most of the ones who haven't are trying to make a profit out of it.

I can't pretend to look down my nose at them. They may have no real choice to do otherwise, but what choice do we have anymore? I don't think anyone's really trying to win now. They're just trying to maintain the illusion that we have some bargaining chip still to play against the North Vietnamese. The war protesters (who are right about some things but not about everything) wouldn't mind if we left altogether. But Nixon still needs the support of his hardcore conservative base, and those are the people he's really trying to deceive (or at least lull into the belief that we're accomplishing something). In reality, we aren't, but for this pull-out to work, he needs to keep them thinking that we are. I don't know if there's any realistic alternative.

I'm really looking forward to seeing you soon.

Love,

Mike

Sgt. Michael Ward

Fire Support Base Las Vegas

Republic of Vietnam

February 19, 1971

Dear Jane,

I'm sorry I wasn't there to help with your scare. At least things turned out okay in the long run. It made me think of Lt. Fitzsimmons' not being there with his wife for the birth of their first child. It will end for us like it did for them. Please let me know how things are going otherwise. Thank you for your assurances about your friend.

I've been thinking about winter lately. You're probably sick and tired of it by now, but I can get nostalgic about funny things. I think what it would be like to wear corduroys and a sweater. I also think about putting on heavy socks with boots to walk in the snow.

Enough of that! I'm on the noon-to-midnight shift now. We'll be having dinner soon, which is served at about four thirty here. After that, we'll be taking the calls from the infantry units in the field with the grid coordinates of their night defensive positions and their defensive targets. Then we will practice "shooting in" the latter.

Love,

Mike

Sgt. Michael Ward

Fire Support Base Las Vegas

Republic of Vietnam

February 20, 1971

Dear Sean,

Things got out of hand yesterday with Lt. Miller. Delta Company walked into an ambush almost as soon as it left its NDP. They called for a danger close contact fire mission. "Danger close" means within 400 meters of friendly forces. Miller appeared to be asleep and didn't respond at all to the radio call. I had to call up the battery adjust to the exec post. He hadn't shown any sign of life by the time we had the white phosphorus data worked up, so I called that up to the guns as well.

For some reason, when that first shot went out, he suddenly sprang to life and started yelling, "Who authorized that shot?" He was a maniac, but we had no time to lose once the forward observer called back, "Repeat H E on the deck." With a live ambush in progress, I had to call up the high-explosive data immediately. Miller kept shouting, "You'll be court-martialed for this!" Then he ran out and yelled, "I'm going to tell the captain."

Of course, Capt. Reynolds could certainly tell it had been my voice on the horn and not Miller's, but if Miller makes enough of a fuss, he could get us both in trouble. It is a clear violation of army regulations for data to be sent to the firing battery without first being approved by an officer. What we have going for us is that we totally broke up the attack on Delta Company. Battalion can be funny, though. I'll keep you posted.

As ever,

Mike

Mrs. Patrick Ward

Jersey City, New Jersey

February 22, 1971

Michael dear,

Today is George Washington's Birthday, so there's no school. The weather wasn't good enough to go down the shore. It rarely is this time of year. We had a nice dinner last night at The Alps. Saw the Fitzgeralds there. They just smiled and said, "Counting down!"

I read an article in the paper yesterday. Then I read it again. Everyone knows we are Vietnamizing and getting our own soldiers out, so what is our government doing to prepare the Vietnamese? It's building them a big prison for $400,000. Apparently, that money goes further than it does here. They're using prison labor at fifty-five cents per week. Is this going to be our legacy? Who do they think is going to be in those cells? Maybe they want them to be nice and comfortable!

Lots of love,

Mom

Sgt. Michael Ward

Fire Support Base Las Vegas

Republic of Vietnam

February 25, 1971

Dear Mom & Dad,

Did I read the news correctly? Did President Nixon really hint last week that now that the US is withdrawing from the war, South Vietnam might undertake an invasion of North Vietnam on its own? Is he losing touch with reality, or does he think the rest of the world already has?

In another part of the military universe, a white army captain who had begun a tour of duty in Okinawa only eighteen days earlier was transferred back to Washington for refusing to shake hands with a black officer. The white officer had received a direct commission, so he hadn't gone to OCS or taken ROTC. He had previously worked for a congressman from

Louisiana. That congressman set up a press conference to defend the captain's actions! What made this story stand out even more was that it was in the same issue of *Stars and Stripes* where the Pentagon denied that an all-volunteer army would also be all black. Like the Defense Department, I think that's unlikely, but what would people like the congressman and the captain do then?

Things have been kind of quiet here lately. Now if they can only stay that way for another month or so!

Love,

Mike

Sgt. Michael Ward

Fire Support Base Las Vegas

Republic of Vietnam

February 27, 1971

Dear Jane,

The congressional probe into military corruption in Vietnam keeps getting worse. Now we have a senior NCO taking the Fifth Amendment thirteen times and refusing to testify about bribery in the PX system. Then a brigadier general denies accepting expensive gifts from a suspected crook in the face of contrary evidence. One of the allegations against this supposed crook is that he was paying PX managers to get them to buy beer from his company.

Reading about this reminded me of some beer that arrived at our so-called club here. It came in old, heavy metal cans I haven't seen for years. I remember when you were considered strong if you could crush a beer can in your hand. With the new cans, a child could do that. This beer came in the old cans, however, and was as flat as tap water. There's no way of avoiding the likelihood that somebody made loads of money selling way-out-of-date beer to the military, which eventually ended up out here with us. I wonder what they were drinking when we were handed this dishpan water.

I'm just going to have to stop thinking about it. It gets me too angry. Most of us gave up a lot to come here, as you well know! I can't absorb how anyone who had ever worn the uniform could sink so low to line his own pockets by passing off crap like this to guys who are actually fighting the war. It wouldn't even surprise me now if those rear-echelon entrepreneurs went home with more medals than the guys stepping around land mines in the jungle.

Love,

Mike

Patrick Ward

Jersey City, New Jersey

February 27, 1971

Dear Mike,

I was reading today an open letter from a former college professor to President Brewster of Yale University. In the letter, he questions whether alumni will keep making donations to the school when Yale may not be worth saving! While I do not agree with the contents of letter, it does make interesting reading, if for no other reason other than to gain insight into some people's thinking.

His complaints are: 1) The university accepts too much money from the government, to the point that its academic freedom is restricted; 2) coeducational classrooms and dormitories cause so much distraction that they curtail academic excellence; 3) students can still obtain financial aid even when their parents refuse to support their objectionable lifestyle; 4) big-time sports go far beyond developing a sound body to house a sound mind; and 5) honorary degrees should not be given to non-scholars.

I will comment on just a couple of them, starting with the last. Everyone in the academic and business world recognizes that an honorary degree given to a graduation speaker is not a real educational accomplishment. It's nothing more than what it claims to be, an honor. With respect to the second item, all my classes over the past few years have been coeducational, and the academic quality has not fallen in the least. I think what we see in the letter is more a protest against changing mores than a critical analysis of the university.

Your mother would like some Italian food tonight, so we are going to Bruno's. I'm sure he will want to hear all about how you are doing. You don't have very long to go. Stay on your toes.

Affectionately,

Dad

Mrs. Patrick Ward

Hudson City, New Jersey

March 1, 1971

Michael dear,

I read a letter in the paper today all full of darkness and doom. It started by referring to a false nuclear alert that occurred on February 20. It then went on to say the invasion of Laos is a failure, the Paris peace negotiations have been practically abandoned, and President Nixon has predicted that South Vietnam will invade North Vietnam. Such an invasion would cause China to enter the war, it said, and once China was in the war, nuclear weapons would be used and we could have a real nuclear alert in the near future. He may be right about the first three things, but the others are a real stretch.

I'm getting excited about the likelihood of your coming home soon. I'm not at all worried about the possibility of your being attacked by a nuclear missile once you get here.

Lots of love,

Mom

Sgt. Michael Ward

Fire Support Base Las Vegas

Republic of Vietnam

March 7, 1971

Dear Jane,

It's been a little while since I heard from you. I guess the mail is backed up again—not unusual. How you are making out after your scare? Will you need any further treatment beyond the aspiration? Do you need a more thorough checkup? I might be home in a month or so. I won't have much to do, since it's too late to start the semester at law school, so I should be able to take you anyplace you need to go. Let me know!

Love,

Mike

Sgt. Michael Ward

Fire Support Base Las Vegas

Republic of Vietnam

March 8, 1971

Dear Mom & Dad,

A retired colonel appeared recently before a Senate committee in Washington investigating bribery and corruption in the military club and recreation system in Vietnam. He testified that contending with crooked profiteers in Long Binh took up more of his time and effort than the Viet Cong. When he tried to do something about the prostitutes at the bath houses on the army base, he was first offered bribes. When he refused those, he was threatened.

That really bugs me. If nothing else, people back home who read about this probably think facilities like that are typical of what life is like for soldiers here. It sure isn't like that for us. I don't think even Chu Lai has anything like that. Even though we all know corporations make profits selling supplies to the military, we understand that's just the way it is. There's no way to avoid some war profiteering. However, when most of us are enduring what we have to for the sake of serving our country, it drives me crazy that some well-placed people can just sit back, profit off the whole thing, and laugh off what the real soldiers are doing. I also think there's a lot more stuff going on than we know. If the Vietnamese are so willing to accept MPCs, which theoretically they can't use anywhere, then someone is changing them for them. Probably for a cut.

Back a couple of months ago, I was coming back from Chu Lai in a truck that had our battalion number painted on the bumper. Just as we were leaving, a soldier none of us knew hopped on the truck and asked to ride back with us. He told us he belonged to the Ninety-Fifth Artillery but never mentioned Charlie Battery. It's like all he did was read the number off the bumper. He was unarmed, which is strange, but he also had two big bags containing cartons of Salem cigarettes. GIs don't smoke all that many Salems, but the Vietnamese love them. They're popular on the black market. Well, as we were going through the village of An Tan, he jumped off the truck and disappeared. Of course, he was just a small fry.

As ever,

Mike

Mrs. Patrick Ward

Jersey City, New Jersey

March 9, 1971

Michael dear,

Easter is going to be on April 11 this year. If what has been happening with your friends is any indication, you should be home by then. I'm planning on having a real Easter Sunday celebration with baked ham, sweet potatoes, and champagne. We'll invite relatives from both sides of the family. I hope you'll be here in time to get some new clothes beforehand, but even if you're not, you still have enough civilian clothes in your closet. You won't have to wear your uniform.

I think it would be better to do it up here in Jersey City rather than down the shore. This location would be more central for some of the people. I just can't wait for the first day of spring, although the weather so far is not hinting at its arrival. It will come, though, and so will you. It won't be long now.

Lots of love,

Mom

Patrick Ward

Jersey City, New Jersey

March 11, 1971

Dear Mike,

The United States Court of Appeals for the Third Circuit handed down a very interesting decision yesterday. It concerned Samuel DeCavalcante (Sam the Plumber), a reputed mob boss in New Jersey. He had been convicted of conspiracy to commit extortion, based on his mediating a dispute between two opposing groups of miscreants. It seems one gang had cheated the other in a dice game, which caused the second gang to demand its money back at gunpoint, and then some, from the cheaters. Both contingents agreed to having Mr. DeCavalcante arbitrate their differences. This was the basis of his trial court conviction. The appellate court held that simply acting as a negotiator between two opposing parties, even where the underlying facts were "unsavory," was insufficient to establish the crime charged.

Both your mother and I are looking forward to seeing you soon. She is starting to make all sorts of plans again, which she hasn't done in a while. It's like she's been in cold storage for the past ten months. Just be careful. While you don't have long to go, a lot of people have already left, and your troop strength is not what it was.

Affectionately,

Dad

Sgt. Michael Ward

Fire Support Base Las Vegas

Republic of Vietnam

March 12, 1971

Dear Sean,

I'm still not sure what Lt. Miller is up to. He's been to see the captain a few times, and people have heard raised voices on both sides. Miller may be waiting for a chance to get into battalion HQ to talk there directly. He's not accomplishing much here.

As our situation continues to deteriorate, I can't help but think of all the guys who've been killed or seriously wounded. In previous wars, they would have been honored and respected. If they died, the whole community gathered around their families in support. If they lived with whatever had happened to them, the same support went to them. In this war, no matter how much a person suffers, no matter how much he sacrifices, no matter how much he believes in what he is doing, the recognition just isn't there. Sure, the war dead receive a military funeral, but the community acts more like his life was wasted than that he died for a cause. Those who live with a severe wound are appreciated by the military community, but not really by the young people of whom they would otherwise be a part.

How did this happen? I know me. I know what I'm like, and I know the guys I'm here with. We're basically the same as those good guys who fought World War II (in many cases, our fathers and their friends). Why can't anybody see that anymore? Sure, there were bad things that happened, but the number of our soldiers who were involved in that is such a small percentage. Most of us came here at great cost to our own personal ambitions, not to mention the toll it took on our relationships. I'm sorry to bother you with this, but I can't say it to anyone else right now.

As ever,

Mike

Sgt. Michael Ward

Fire Support Base Las Vegas

Republic of Vietnam

March 14, 1971

Dear Mom & Dad,

Doug Grayson received his orders to go home today. That's really good news, since he got here only a couple of weeks before I did. He's a very pleasant guy from eastern Pennsylvania, a Villanova graduate. I gave him your phone number, and he's going to try to call you. He got drafted so quickly after college he didn't even have time to look for a job. He's our FADAC operator here. Maybe that will help him, as most people think computers are going to be used more and more as time goes on. He gets along with everybody, so he should do well on an interview.

I have to believe this means my orders will be coming soon.

We've already had dinner, even though it's only 5:15. Time to start working on our defensive targets—but not for that much longer now!

Love,

Mike

Mrs. Patrick Ward

Jersey City, New Jersey

March 16, 1971

Michael dear,

I'm getting so excited. Your room is neat as a pin, just waiting for your arrival. Everyone we meet on the street, in restaurants, wherever, all ask when the big day will be. We have to tell them we don't know yet, but it will be soon. I don't even know if this letter will reach you in time.

Your father wants to take a picture of you at the airport in your uniform. You won't be wearing it much longer now. Do you have a credit card to pay for your airfare from Seattle to Newark? I know the army will give you a travel allowance in cash, but a card would be easier.

Please telephone us as soon as you are able. I don't know how easy it is to make telephone calls from Fort Lewis. Your friends and your family will give you a big welcome home whether the rest of the country wants to join in or not.

Lots of love,

Mom

Jane O'Brien

Jersey City, New Jersey

March 17, 1971

Dear Michael,

Where do I begin? I'm sorry to say this, but I'm not your girlfriend anymore. I desperately want you to come home safely, but we're not on the same page. It doesn't have anything to do with attitudes about the war—yours, mine, or anyone else's—although I'm still dumbfounded by what happened at My Lai and at Kent State. These were not oversights or administrative mistakes, but that's not the point.

I needed you here, not halfway around the world, and it's not just this past year. Your first year in the army, all we got were two leaves. I needed a boyfriend, not a pen pal. I had to rely on other people—other people who, yes, may have avoided the draft. They were here for me, though.

But that's not the really sad thing. The really sad thing is you could have been here. Why weren't you? Some misplaced sense of nobility? Michael, this isn't World War II. You're not defeating the Nazis. As a matter of fact, you're not defeating anybody! No one would have criticized you if you'd served in the Army Reserve. A lot of people say those men are being saved for the real war with the Russians, anyway.

If you wanted to be really noble, you should have been more concerned about me and your poor mother. You think I was upset by what you did? Let me tell you, she was much more upset than I was. She just hid it better. She remembers what happened last time all too well. Her husband came home, but her brother didn't. How do you think she really feels? She won't say it in her letters.

I still want to see you, but it won't be like before. I'll be going to Florida with some of the other teachers for spring break. You may not want to hear it from me anymore, but happy St. Patrick's Day. At least you're wearing the right color clothes for that.

Love always,

Jane

Chapter 12
SAPPERS

Sgt. Michael Ward

Fire Support Base Las Vegas

Republic of Vietnam

March 17, 1971

Dear Jane,

Happy St. Patrick's Day! I wish I were there to share it with you, but since I can't be, I decided to send you something. Hai, the girl who works in the laundry, has another more conventional sideline business selling artifacts her sister makes. Her vases are really nice. They are actually made of paper-mache, but they're so smooth and hard they seem like ceramic. Most of them show scenes of people in conical hats paddling boats past grass cottages and palm trees.

I had this one made specially. I lent her that picture I took of you in South Carolina last year holding up the fish you caught, still on the pole. As you can see, I had her make the fish a little bigger. No one would have been able to see it if she hadn't! I've kept the picture with me and look at it all the time. (Not to admire the fish.) Now you have a handcrafted version.

Love,

Mike

Sgt. Michael Ward

Fire Support Base Las Vegas

Republic of Vietnam

March 20, 1971

Dear Mom & Dad,

It can't be much longer now. Once Doug leaves tomorrow, there will be no one here from when I arrived. That gives me a certain amount of prestige. Among the lower ranks, people are more impressed by your time in country than by your rank.

Spring is a nice time to be going home, even it's not convenient for school. We won't have beach weather for a while, but it should be nice for golf by the time I get there. The prospect looks good for getting home by Easter. I would certainly not want to spoil your plans. Not all the drops are uniform. Some people get a little more time off than others. A lot has to do with how many seats are available on the flights. They fill up the planes as they become available.

I don't know how much you're following what's happening in Laos, but it appears that the North Vietnamese are now using tanks and artillery against the South Vietnamese. That's something they couldn't do if we were there. Our own artillery could take out theirs without much difficulty, and their armor too. Is this a foreshadowing of what it's going to be like in South Vietnam once we leave?

Love,

Mike

Sean Ward

Jersey City, New Jersey

March 22, 1971

Hey Mike,

I'm sorry to say this, but this recent Laotian fiasco appears to have put the last nail in the coffin of whatever credibility Nixon's program of Vietnamization still had remaining. We don't even seem to be able to get the troops out that we sent in. Some South Vietnamese commanders are admitting that the size of the force sent into Laos was inadequate, but they're claiming they couldn't send any more without dangerously weakening their own defenses. All of this is despite the fact that they still have American forces in Vietnam. What are they going to do when those US troops are gone? It's fine to have peace talks in Paris, but what do we have to negotiate with anymore? I'm glad you won't be there much longer.

I saw Jane shopping on Bergen Avenue the other day. She did her best to avoid me, and she hasn't been peppering me with questions the way she used to for some time now. Don't let it get to you. You'll be coming home very soon. What you do then is your business. You can try to repair that relationship or just move on. You guys did seem like a good match, but the country you left is not the one you'll be returning to. She already knows that. On a positive note, you won't be stuck on a remote firebase, either. Whatever's going on, you'll be back in the mix. You haven't been for some time.

Take care of yourself,

Sean

Sgt. Michael Ward

Fire Support Base Las Vegas

Republic of Vietnam

March 23, 1971

Dear Sean,

I have to admit to feeling uneasy. Things are just too quiet here. We haven't had an incident since that guard at the entrance was found dead four months ago. As a result of the drop in the length of tours, almost half the guys here have arrived since then and seem to think the war is over. It's not. Ten months isn't a lot of time, but I've seen things heat up here very quickly without warning. I'm not the only one trying to encourage the new guys to stay on their toes, but they still seem to think the NVA and Viet Cong are just going to sit back and wait for us to leave before they do anything. That's dangerous.

The home front doesn't seem to be any better. It's hard to keep up with all the articles on antiwar activities. First I see those Green Berets who parachuted into North Adams Airport in Massachusetts got surrounded by hundreds of college students *and faculty* shouting obscenities at them and asking how many people they had killed. Those people should stop and think about that. They may need defending someday. And then the Council of Churches in New York canceling plans to honor Bob Hope—Bob Hope! Isn't this getting a little ridiculous?

I'm no war hero, but this hasn't been an easy year. At the very least, I wouldn't want to be disrespected for it, and there are people who've had it a lot worse than I have. When I first came here, even antiwar protesters were lining up to donate blood to soldiers. Would they still do that?

As ever,

Mike

(Translation)

People's Army of Vietnam

Region 5

Headquarters

March 24, 1971

To: Commander, 407th Viet Cong Main Force Sapper Battalion:

1. It has been determined by this command that the people's forces are to move against the military base at Chu Lai once it is turned over to the Army of the Republic of Vietnam by the Americans.

2. In order to do this, the people's forces must first have control of the surrounding area, which the Americans refer to as the Rocket Pocket.

3. That area is presently patrolled by the Fifth Battalion of the American Forty-Sixth Infantry Regiment, 198th Light Infantry Brigade, Americal Division.

4. For the past two months, we have staged numerous ambushes to destroy the effectiveness of that unit.

5. This program was proving successful initially because of significant delays in the responding artillery fire from Battery C, Second Battalion of the Ninety-Fifth Artillery Regiment, Americal Division.

6. Those delays were permitting our forces to inflict substantial casualties before being forced to withdraw.

7. Recently, however, that battery's response time has been shortened back to effective levels to the point that our forces' engagements are no longer productive.

8. All of our recent ambushes have been thwarted by fire from that battery.

9. It is essential to destroy the operational capability of that artillery battery for our plan to control the Rocket Pocket to succeed.

10. The battery's guns are located on three separate firebases but all are controlled by the fire direction center at Fire Support Base Las Vegas.

11. You are to conduct a major sapper attack on that firebase quickly to destroy that fire direction center and all its personnel.

ON THE AUTHORITY OF THE COMMANDER

Sgt. Michael Ward

Fire Support Base Las Vegas

Republic of Vietnam

March 26, 1971

Dear Mom & Dad,

My orders for going home have arrived. The date I'm scheduled to leave Vietnam is April 6. I am enclosing a copy of the orders. They certainly gave me enough copies of them. Since I'll be leaving this firebase in only three days, you can tell everyone to stop writing. I'll be there to receive any and all news personally.

It will probably seem a little strange at first with so

many of my old friends moved away or married. The situation with Jane is something else. Not only did we start out on a bad foot, but the environment she was in was worse than nonsupportive. It was downright antagonistic toward the military and anyone associated with us. I now realize there's nothing I can do about it without being there. Look for me about April 10.

Love,

Mike

ORDERS

FOR THE INDIVIDUAL

Sergeant Michael Ward

Assigned to: USARV Returnee Detachment 2 April 1971

Reporting date to proper Returnee Detachment: 3 April 1971

Report to 22d Replacement Battalion not later than 48 hours and not earlier than 72 hours prior to 6 April 71 for the purpose of processing and onward movement to McChord AFB, WA. Report to 22d Replacement Battalion, Cam Ranh Bay, for further assignment to USATRFSTA, Ft. Lewis, WA 98433 for separation.

Harold Chrisom

Colonel, GS

Chief of Staff

Mrs. David O'Brien

Jersey City, New Jersey

March 26, 1971

Dear Jane,

    This letter and package from Mike in Vietnam arrived today. I thought you might want to see it before you come home from Florida.

Love,

Mom

Sgt. Michael Ward

Fire Support Base Las Vegas

Republic of Vietnam

March 27, 1971

Dear Sean,

    I had to go into Chu Lai today to clear up some paperwork for my departure. That's not important. What is important is that on the way back, I hitched a ride on a truck bound for Tam Ky. It dropped me off at the intersection of Route 1 and our dirt road. I had started walking when one of the kids we found in the bush nine months ago appeared suddenly at the edge. He kept looking around and wouldn't walk out onto the roadway. He spoke very low and said, "This night, sappas come this night." Then he slipped back into the brush.

It sounded like he was saying that we were going to have a sapper attack tonight. Why would he tell us this? Maybe a lot of South Vietnamese do support us, even if they can't do so openly. Obviously I had to tell Capt. Reynolds about this, even if I had to waver a little on how the kid knew me. There's not much Reynolds can do, though, and the infantry lieutenant was totally unimpressed by my story. He thought it was nonsense to believe a kid like that. I don't know what I can do, but I'll keep you posted.

I'm going to make sure this letter goes out today. The last truck is leaving shortly.

Will get back to you soon,

Mike

Jane O'Brien

Seaview Hotel

Ft. Lauderdale, Florida

March 27, 1971

Dear Michael,

Thank you for the vase. If it wasn't so clear that you'd sent it before you got my letter, I'd accuse you of trying to make things even harder than they had to be. I realize you did send it before you heard from me, but what's more important is that you kept that photograph with you so long.

I'm sorry, but I still don't understand how you could have left me just to participate in that ridiculous charade masquerading as a war. Believe me, I've so tried to understand your feelings, but somehow I always get lost in the "How could you?" and "Do you really feel as I do?"

Don't make the mistake of thinking Jeremy is the problem. The problem has to do with us. He's here at this hotel, as well as three of the other teachers, but I don't think I realized how much of a pompous ass he was until having to put up with him at every meal. I'm sorry, I meant "intelligent pompous ass." Do you remember when Eddie came up from Washington the summer of '67 when we first started dating? He tried to impress you by reciting passages from Joyce's *Ulysses,* and I had to run to the ladies room to keep from bursting out at the expression on your face. Well, Jeremy has a lot in common with Eddie. Whatever our problems, even if we can't resolve them, he could never replace you. When are you coming home?

Love,

Jane

NEWS REPORT
March 28, 1971

Saigon—There are reports that the United States Army may have suffered disastrous losses last night at an artillery position known as Fire Support Base Las Vegas. Early information indicates that massive explosions, including large napalm fireballs, could be seen from as far away as Chu Lai. Fighting is still ongoing. Parts of the base are believed to be in enemy hands. Helicopter gunships cannot fire because of the uncertainty of which bunkers are under American control. Further reports will be forthcoming.

Jane O'Brien

Seaview Hotel

Ft. Lauderdale, Florida

March 28, 1971

Dear Mr. & Mrs. Ward,

I've tried calling you. Do you know anything about what happened at Fire Support Base Las Vegas? There are news reports. Have you heard anything about Michael? Please call my parents' house if you learn anything. Even if you haven't heard anything, I would want to know that.

    I can't just do nothing. Why did I have to send that stupid letter? Michael and I may have had our difficulties, but that wasn't the way to handle them. I had already waited almost two years. All I had to do was to wait one lousy little month more.

I can't blame the people around me, even if they were no help. I can't blame them for staying out of the army, either. I just wish they didn't think that made them brighter and more clever than anyone who did otherwise. Michael did warn me to be wary of people whose principles compel them to do whatever is easiest for them.

But none of that is what I'm scared of. I don't want my walking out the door of Luigi's to have been the last time he ever saw me. I don't want my St. Patrick's Day letter to have been the last time he ever heard from me. I tried to write him again, but that was the same day as the attack.

I promise to keep you informed. The school board will just have to sit this one out.

Love,

Jane

NEWS REPORT
March 29, 1971

Saigon—Reports from Chu Lai indicate that fighting continues at Fire Support Base Las Vegas. There are no casualty reports yet.

Jane O'Brien

Colonial Hotel

Saigon

Republic of Vietnam

April 1, 1971

Dear Mr. & Mrs. Ward,

As you can see, I made it here. After writing to you, I changed my return flight and got one to Kennedy Airport. From there, I was able to get another flight to San Francisco and then to Anchorage, Alaska, then to Tokyo and then to Tan Son Nhut. I was able to get into the Military Assistance Command today, but I haven't been able to learn anything more than what the news reports are already saying. The only way I'm going to find out anything is to get to Chu Lai some-how. I will let you know anything I learn.

Love,

Jane

CWO Richard Davenport

Fifty-Fourth Medical Detachment

Helicopter Ambulance

Chu Lai

Republic of Vietnam

April 2, 1971

Dear Sheila,

This has been a rough day. Americal Division head-quarters had to bring another whole battalion into the Rocket Pocket to try to retake Firebase Las Vegas. It was more than just a sapper attack; the sappers were backed up by infantry. Our reinforcements finally had the enemy cleared out by nine o'clock this morning. Then we started having to move the wounded out. It was the worst carnage I've seen in the eight months I've been here. We had four dust-off helicopters work-ing, and I still had to make six runs.

A strange thing happened in Chu Lai. There was a young American woman in civilian clothes who insisted on checking all the patients. She came up to me every time I landed with a new batch. All the pilots had that experience with her. By my last run, she was frantic (not surprising, considering all the gore she had seen), but then she began wiping blood off one man's face and sobbing, "Michael, Michael, Michael." Then she followed the stretcher bearers into the hospital.

All I kept thinking was what would it be like if I were the man on the stretcher and you were that woman.

Love,

Rich

Sgt. Michael Ward

Second Surgical Hospital

Chu Lai

Republic of Vietnam

April 4, 1971

Dear Mom & Dad,

The medic had me so shot full of morphine I thought I must be dreaming, dreaming that I was lying on a stretcher on the ground and Jane was wiping blood off my face—but no, I wasn't dreaming. She's here now.

I know she already wrote you from Saigon. From there, she boarded a C-130 to Chu Lai. They asked her name but nothing else. I guess they assumed she was a Red Cross Donut Dolly or a USO worker. As long as she was an American woman, they didn't care. It's not like flying a civilian airline with tickets.

You must have heard at least something from the army by now. It looks like they'll be able to save my leg. They say there'll be some issues, though, especially with my eyesight.

Fortunately, the FDC held. Thank you, God! I wrote in my last letter to Sean that I'd been told by a very nervous Vietnamese kid to expect trouble that night. I passed it on to our commander, but there wasn't much he could do, and the infantry commander thought my story was ridiculous.

But I had an idea. When I first got there, our base

held a lot more people, and we had perimeter spotlights
that worked off our generator. They were let go as our
numbers decreased. Leonard Beaver, my Seminole friend,
is our new generator operator and had been working
with Capt. Reynolds to get them set up again, but they
weren't operational yet. I asked Leonard if he could have
any spotlights in place by nightfall, and he said he could
get three of them working. Capt. Reynolds agreed. We
decided to place them on the south perimeter, since that's
the direction previous sapper attacks have come from.
My shift was off duty from noon to midnight, so we all
helped, even my usually uncooperative "friend." It was all
done by dark, and we went back to the FDC bunker and
made sure all our equipment, weapons, and ammo were
in place.

Leonard agreed to throw the light switch on at
ten o'clock. We were all in position outside the bunker
behind the dirt-filled wooden ammunition box barri-
cades when he did. We'd hoped the lights would scare off
any attackers, but when they came on, they illuminated
sappers already coming through the wire plus infantry in
position on the outside to back them up.

Fortunately, one of our infantry guards in a perimeter bunker had enough presence of mind to squeeze the
handle on the fougasse trigger, which sent out a flaming wave of napalm that knocked out a good part of the
attacking force. We were able to hold off the remaining attackers from the FDC bunker, but some of the
other bunkers didn't do as well, especially those nearer
the perimeter.

For over five days, we appeared to be at a stalemate, with each side controlling part of the firebase. We couldn't even get air or artillery support, since they had no way of knowing if they were shooting at friendly or hostile positions. Division headquarters had to send an infantry battalion to relieve us on the ground.

When that battalion closed in, the sappers made a last-ditch effort to take the FDC by throwing satchel charges over our barricade. That's how I got wounded. I wouldn't be alive but for our fire direction officer. For almost all the battle, Lt. Miller stayed inside looking like he was in a near coma, but when the first satchel charges of the final attack went off, he rushed out with his .45 blazing. He hit two of the sappers carrying satchel charges. They fell, and the charges went off outside our barricade, killing the sappers and, unfortunately, Lt. Miller.

I didn't expect my war to end this way. We were all very well intentioned coming here. I'm not sure that communism or capitalism has anything to do with it. Neither of the two Vietnamese governments are really tied to either of those systems. What we were facing was an attempt by the north to take over the south. There are both ethnic and linguistic differences between the Cochinchinese and the Tonkinese peoples.

Defending the south would be morally acceptable, had we approached it sensibly, but our strategy wasn't realistic. Even leaving aside the lack of any ground-gaining initiative, we never mobilized our reserve forces. We kept the two-year draft and one-year combat tour, which prevented us from developing seasoned troops. The constant rotation of personnel kept soldiers from learning to work together as a team. Even worse, we limited command time to six months, forcing our small unit leaders to rotate out just as they were finally getting the hang of it. I still don't understand why our infantry, who spoke no Vietnamese and had no understanding of Vietnamese village life, had to take local patrols over from the South Vietnamese Army, which had both of those advantages.

After the Cambodia thing fell flat on its face, I don't think anyone below the rank of lieutenant colonel was even pretending to try to win the war, and those above that rank were doing just that—pretending. What we were really trying to do was to stay alive and keep each other as safe as possible. I looked on our artillery fire as a way of protecting the infantry.

I can't wait to go home and back to law school, but most of all, I just want to be back in the United States with all the other Americans, hippies and hard hats, hawks and doves, all of us finally realizing that in this crazy world, we have to stick together.

They're going to move me to Japan soon to a US military hospital there. Jane can't fly with me, so she'll take a civilian flight to Tokyo. She says she refuses to go home without me, and I assured her I will never leave her ever again.

Love,

Mike

Now that you have finished reading Firebase, please consider leaving a review online

ACKNOWLEDGMENTS

Since this novel is in epistolary form, consisting mostly of letters, the first people I wish to thank are those who wrote to me in the army from whose letters I got much of my inspiration. I would start with my parents Joy and Mark Sullivan, my godmother Margy McFarland, my aunt Margie Shay, my aunt Meave Reilly, my aunt Marge Sullivan, my aunt and uncle Jim and Eileen Cotter, my aunt and uncle Joe and Polly Sullivan. My cousins Gael Connell, Eileen Cotter Malouf, Mary Elizabeth Cotter, Diane Fischl Swift, Maeve Ostrowski, Meave Poden Foley, Ellen Shay Roumasset, Isabel Shay Milazzo, Cathy Sullivan von Lengerke, Dee Sullivan Yost, Arthur McGuire, Mickey Reilly, Mary Ellen Sullivan and Harry McFarland. There were also Ginny Blasi, Brian Sheeran, Isidore Hornstein, Beth Cangemi, Pat Donnelly, Michele Eppler, Maryann Fischl, Joanne Kenny, Bill Schaaf, Mike Schattman, Paul Maloy, Connie Schaaf, Shelley Pangaro, Bob Cheloc, Al Oates, Peter Artaserse and John Small. (Feel free to let me know if I missed anyone as I was working from a stack of 47-year-old letters in the basement.)

I especially want to thank my friends and relatives who read over my rough drafts, and gave me much needed advice. My fellow retired judge Jack Tassini and my cousin Roro Poden gave me many good pointers. There was much good advice from my wife Marlene and from my daughter Mary Beth. I also received help from my cousins Maeve Ostrowski, Diane Fischl Swift and John Shay and from Richard Kenah, an air force veteran of Southeast Asia. I further want to thank Sgt. Clarence Marrs for maintaining the battery website for Charlie Battery, 1st of the Fourteenth Artillery, the unit in which I served. Its photos brought back a lot of memories that made writing easier.